Very Good Nov. 12–15

D0876399

This book is on loan from the
Mid York Library System

When you are finished reading,
please return the book so
that others may enjoy it.

The Mid York Library System is pleased to
partner with **CABVI** in assisting those with
special vision needs. If you found the size
of print in this book helpful, there may be other
ways **CABVI** can help. Please call today toll
free at **1-877-719-9996** or **(315) 797-2233**.

MID YORK *Library System*

0 Lincoln Avenue Utica, New York 13502

VIOLET WINSPEAR

the loved and the feared

G.K.HALL &CO.
Boston, Massachusetts
1983

Copyright © 1977 by Violet Winspear. All rights reserved.
Philippine copyright 1980. Australian copyright 1980.

Published in Large Print by arrangement with
Mills & Boon, Ltd.

Set in 16 pt English Times.

Library of Congress Cataloging in Publication Data

Winspear, Violet.
  The loved and the feared.

  ''Published in large print''—T.p. verso.
  1. Large type books. I. Title.
[PR6073.I5543L65 1983]   823'.914   83-12783
ISBN 0-8161-3566-5 (lg. print)

Chapter One

The fascination of the scenery held Donna Lovelace enthralled, with its narrow roads hacked out of the hillsides and winding upwards all the way until the rackety cab seemed to hang in the air above the great clumps of rock and the deep gleam of the sea. The Italian driver of the cab seemed entirely nerveless, blasting his horn most of the time and hurling remarks at Donna that she barely understood but took to be reassurances that they weren't about to plunge over the cliffs.

The craggy hillsides were swept by sun and wind and Donna had the feeling that civilisation was being left on the lower slopes of southern Italy, along with the terraced vines and the silvery-grey olive trees; the mulberries and almonds. Up here there was a wildness and a grandeur that excited her even as it alarmed her.

When the driver suddenly flung the words, 'Villa Imperatore!' over his shoulder she felt

1

her heart quicken with anticipation and knew they were nearing her destination.

Somehow she hadn't expected the villa of Serafina Neri to be in this part of Italy. She had imagined it in the smart suburbs of Rome, an elegant *palazzo* in a park, with white statues agleam in the sun and fountains spraying. A house in this high region would surely be more primitive . . . even romantic.

The cab swept around a bend in the precarious road and there ahead of them were tall iron gates that were firmly closed. The cab screeched to a halt and a uniformed guard strolled out of a small stone house set among a group of trees; he came to the gates to exchange a barrage of Italian with Donna's driver.

After several minutes the driver turned to her and said excitedly: 'Passport, mees! Show passport, *avanti!*'

'Oh—he wants to make sure I'm genuine?' Donna flipped open her bag, extracted her passport and handed it over. The guard then took a number of minutes to scrutinise the picture inside and finally requested that Signorina Lovelace be so good as to step from the vehicle so he could make sure of her identity.

Donna did as she was asked and had the feeling she had reached the frontier of some Ruritanian principality ruled over by Serafina Neri, the world-famous film star, now retired and living in seclusion, protected by her own

2

special guards not only from photographers and sightseers but from the constant threat of abduction, the menace that wealthy Italians lived with.

They had to be careful, Donna supposed, but surely this guard on the gate could see that she wasn't carrying a camera or a gun. His eyes flicked her up and down, and then he handed back the passport, and spoke again to the cab driver, waving his hands about and obviously quite firm about what he was proposing.

Donna soon learned, for the driver climbed out of the cab, pulled her baggage from the boot, held out his hand and demanded his fare. It seemed that she was to be allowed through the gates, but on foot. The guard obviously had strict orders that he wasn't to trust anyone, and she supposed he felt confident he could deal with a slim young secretary clad in a white shirt and doeskin skirt, a soft leather bag slung from her shoulder, into which he delved the moment he had let her through the gates and bolted them again. The cab drove off in a stampede of dust, and Donna stood there quietly while her bag was searched, her thick wheaten hair held at her nape in a big tortoiseshell slide, her ale-coloured eyes shaded by dark lashes quite innocent of any make-up.

There was a certain independent style to the girl, though she didn't possess any formal sort of beauty. Her nose tilted, her soft scarlet mouth was too wide and crinkly, and there was a crooked little cleft in her chin. Her figure was willowy, the bones clearly defined in her ankles, wrists and collarbones.

She lifted her face to the sun and relished the feel of it. There were aspects to this job at the Villa Imperatore that were strange and decidedly alarming, but she had longed to come to Italy, and had secured this position with La Neri because her father had been a well-known film cameraman who had worked on a couple of Serafina's films and lighted the actress so well and made her look so lovely that La Neri had never forgotten him. She had remembered the name Lovelace, and so Donna was here and about to undertake the task of helping the famous star to write her memoirs.

Donna had freelanced on this sort of work before and preferred it to the routine of office work. It held its perils, of course, and once she had helped a well-known comedian to write his biography and found it decidedly un-funny trying to keep out of his clutches.

But this time she'd be working for a woman, thank goodness, and there was less risk of losing her patience, not to mention her honour, when she finally got down to the job.

'*Grazie.*' She smiled at the guard as she accepted her bag and slung it back on her shoulder. He stared a moment at her, then his mouth relaxed slightly and he bent to pick up her suitcases. He gestured that she follow him and Donna proceeded to do so, along a narrow pathway among the trees that was presumably a short cut to the villa. Birds whistled and hopped upon the branches overhead, adding to the air of seclusion, of an estate deliberately isolated from the rest of the region. What must it feel like, Donna wondered, to be a rich, famous beauty who lived in fear of being kidnapped? Was there a certain excitement in it for a woman who no longer vamped her way across the cinema screen but who lived on past glory, separated from her husband whom she had never divorced because she was a devout Catholic?

The trees suddenly thinned and Donna followed the guard out upon a wide forecourt fronting the Villa Imperatore . . . it was quite wonderful, but in no way a classic Latin villa. Its walls were cobbled, hung with clumps of flowering weed, with a side tower crowned by an archway in which hung a large iron bell. The long main structure was roofed in red oval tiles, with a central archway leading into a small courtyard ablaze with climbing plants, great terracotta pots spilling with flowers, and centred by a fountain with three stone basins into which the water was tumbling, probably fed from one of the mountain streams.

'Fascinating,' Donna murmured. 'Like

something out of a dream.'

'*Scusa, signorina?*' The guard gave her a questioning look.

'*Molto bello,*' she smiled, waving a hand at the villa. '*Buona fortezza.*' Donna had a sense of humour and couldn't always suppress it.

'*Si, si.*' He nodded, understanding her, perhaps at heart a gentle man despite the polished, lethal-looking pistol that hung from his belt. 'Come, *signorina. Andiamo!*'

He walked in under the archway and Donna followed him past the cool splash of the fountain to an oval-shaped wooden door inset with a Judas window. He pulled the iron bell at the side of the little grille, waited until a face appeared at the other side, then nodded and left Donna standing there with her suitcases at her feet.

The dark eyes stared at her through the grille. 'I'm Miss Lovelace,' Donna explained. 'The Signora Neri is expecting me.'

'*Si.*' The wooden door was opened and the slim young footman picked up her baggage and led her across the dim, polished, air-cooled hall and up a flight of stairs to the *salone*. Here the footman paused and tapped upon one of the double doors, casting at the same time a sideglance at Donna that was, she felt, very Italian in its assessment of her face and figure. She remained a trifle aloof, for she already had the feeling that in surrounding herself with men La Neri was probably one of those women who liked to be the centre of their attraction. Flirtations, Donna felt, would not be welcomed in this house, not that she was the type who indulged in them all that frequently. She hadn't yet met the man who could set her pulses thudding and her senses aflame.

'*Avanti!*'

The footman swept open the door and ushered Donna into a lovely, almost barbaric room, so that Donna saw the great sofas upholstered in zebra skin, and the great spread llama skins on the floor of polished wood blocks before she actually looked at the sole occupant of the *salone.*

'The Signorina Lovelace,' intoned the footman, who then withdrew, leaving Donna alone with her employer.

They gazed at each other, a slim fair English girl, and a goddess-like Latin woman with masses of shining dark hair, long lustrous green eyes, an imperious nose and mouth, and a perfect body clad in a jade-green houserobe of shimmering soft silk. La Neri was smoking a cheroot and standing with her back to a long window . . . she was every inch the dream *inamorata* of a million men, and Donna was in no doubt that the Italian woman revelled in her power.

'So you are Donna,' she said, in a rich silky voice, her English made even more attractive by her accent; the voice which had murmured so many endearments while those long, pale hands had caressed in dreams the men who watched her in the darkness of the cinema and tried to pretend that their wives or girlfriends looked as she did.

'Your father, Donna, was a very good friend of mine. He was a fine cameraman, a master of the art, and he knew exactly how to photograph my face so my Italian nose would not look—well, too Italian, if you get my meaning?'

Donna smiled and suddenly realised that this woman was far more human than she appeared at first glance. There was a smile in her lustrous eyes, a curve to her lips as she let the cheroot smoke drift from between them.

'He often spoke of you, Signora Neri. He told me you had more style than any other star he had worked with.'

'*Grazie*. But it saddens me that he died in that awful studio fire in Los Angeles—a great, very sad loss for you, my child, especially in view of having lost your mother when you were so young. However, it is fate the things that happen to us, and we can no more avoid our fate than we can avoid the fall of night and the coming of dawn. So, Donna, you are going to assist me to be an *autore*. It will be a very new role for me, and it will help to pass the time, no?'

Donna smiled as she thought of this vast estate owned by this woman and all the things she could find to do; exploring her domain, finding out all the flowers that grew about the place, all the birds that sang in its trees, all the tracks that led to breathtaking aspects of the mountains and the ocean.

But La Neri was a cosseted orchid, not a rambling rose, and it had probably never occurred to her that there was pleasure to be found in simple things. For too long she had lived in the spotlight and now wanted to put into a book her teaming memories of those days and nights of starry glamour . . . her loves, her triumphs, and her tears.

'Do you think we shall work good together?' An elegant hand made a gesture towards a deep chair and Donna sat down, crossing her slim legs and reposing her hands, with the short unpolished fingernails of the typist.

'I hope so, *signora,*' she replied. 'The villa is a fascinating place and I have a feeling I'm going to enjoy Italy.'

'Everyone who has any heart enjoys Italy.' The cheroot was stubbed and green eyes flicked Donna's legs and simple clothing. 'You will call me Serafina, like everyone else here at the villa. Tell me, have you no young man to object to being parted from you while we work on my memoirs? The book will take time, for I have much to tell, and I don't permit strangers here on visits to my staff.'

'I have no boy-friend—not on a

permanent basis,' Donna said. 'I suppose you could call me a career girl.'

'Good.' Serafina sat down herself on one of the zebra-covered sofas, arranging herself with a natural elegance, so the folds of her robe fell gracefully about her slender, well-cared-for figure. She could easily have passed for a woman in her thirties, yet Donna knew from what her father had told her that La Neri was almost forty-one. It was incredible, and if at any time she had undergone cosmetic surgery there was no sign of it. Her skin was matt and warm-coloured, and she had the luscious kind of mouth that men would crave to kiss.

'You stare at me.' Serafina slowly smiled. 'Are you wondering how ancient I might be when I daresay you know that I have a grown-up son of twenty-five?'

'My father told me you were beautiful,' Donna said, a trifle shyly. 'Real in-the-bone beauty doesn't fade, it just seems to improve in texture.'

'Like an emerald or a Picasso, eh?' Serafina laughed richly. 'If a woman is born beautiful, then she takes care of her beauty, just as she would take care of a precious gem. I rarely go out in the sun, and I daresay that would seem sacrilege to a young, obviously energetic girl like yourself. I never eat starchy foods, nor do I drink wine, though I sometimes enjoy a small cognac. Italian food is fattening, so I leave well alone the *pasta* and the *polenta* and keep strictly to a diet of broiled beefsteak and green vegetables. I am a very vain woman, Donna, and I can also be capricious and cruel when the mood is upon me. Do you think your nerves will stand up to me?'

'I'm no wilting plant—Serafina.' It was a beautiful name, but Donna still felt a trifle shy about using it, especially when she recalled the extraordinary fame of this striking woman, who had risen from the back streets of Sicily to become an international star who had been wooed by some of the world's most eligible men. But Serafina had been married when she was eighteen to a man older than herself, with whom she had lived only a short while, producing a son that he had reared while she had gone off in search of fame and fortune. She had never lived again with her husband and for some strange, private reason of her own had found it convenient to stay married to him. It almost seemed as if she perferred the worship of men to be at a distance . . . like a true goddess of mythology.

'No.' Serafina ran her remarkable eyes over her youthful secretary. 'You have good hair and bones and a certain poise which I like. You are not subservient—I detest and despise people who bow and scrape to me. Ah yes,' the well-cared-for teeth showed in a brilliant smile, 'I like homage, but I like the honest kind, not the kind they call lip service. I have guards about this place. You have seen

11

them, of course. You understand, Donna, that I have wealth and there are *briganti* in the hills of Italy who would like to abduct me for ransom. Once it was tried! I was travelling by car to Naples to visit my sister and they surrounded the car on motor-cycles, but luckily I had with me my personal bodyguard and he was able to get me away from these loathesome, dirty creatures who will not work for a living but prey like vultures on those who have worked for what they have.'

Serafina lounged back against the zebra skin, her dark head at rest against a brilliant cushion, her eyelids half-closed. '*Si,* I have worked like a dog in my time and it will all be told in my memoirs—they will be exciting and for some they will be provoking, for they will reveal the quirks and faults as well as the charms of people I have known. You will not be bored, my young English helper. You may be amused—even made envious by the excitements of my life when I was a girl in my twenties. Tell me, have you yet had a lover?'

'No——' Donna was taken aback by the frankness of the question and felt the hot colour come into her cheeks. 'Not if you mean——?'

'Yes, that is exactly what I mean.' Serafina laughed softly as she studied the lingering colour on Donna's cheekbones. 'I thought all British girls were highly emancipated and only too ready to discard the chastity belt. Why are you different, eh? Have you not yet met a man who stirs you to reckless desire? Is it even possible that you possess old-fashioned ideals, such as saving yourself for your wedding night?'

Donna didn't welcome this kind of probing into her personal life, but she recognised that Serafina might be a rather lonely woman for all her luxury and the protectiveness of her guards. Now that she found herself in the company of another female she obviously felt the compulsion to gossip, and the gossip of women invariably led to the bedroom.

'I've never yet met a man I cared that much for,' Donna admitted. 'I've also kept rather busy since I left business college.'

Serafina probed Donna's face with her green eyes. 'You have unusual looks, though it would not be strictly true to call you pretty. The pale gold hair is natural, eh? I ask because you have such dark lashes in contrast, and also darker toned eyebrows.'

'I couldn't be bothered to be a dyed blonde,' Donna replied. 'Those dark roots would be too much!'

'Proving you have a basic honesty and good sense.' Serafina nodded to herself. 'I think I shall get along with you, Donna, for the most part. I got along very well with your father. We used to share sausage sandwiches on the set, but in those days, of course, I was less in danger of putting on weight. Sausage with a spread of mustard—ah, those sandwiches were really quite delicious. You must miss that nice man very much, child?'

Donna nodded. 'Dad was tough and uncompromising and he probably set an example I look for in—in other men.'

'That is inevitable,' Serafina agreed. 'I much loved my own father, but it will all be told in the book, how he died, leaving my mother to bring up a daughter on her own. I was nice to look at and—and the boys were soon after me. Sicilian girls blossom quickly, you understand, and some of them marry very young— As I did. A kind enough man, but the life with him was too tame, and when I had the chance to enter a beauty contest I took it——'

Serafina spread her hands and her rings glittered on her fingers. 'It was the beginning for me. I won the contest and was given a walk-on part in a film about the rice fields. Ah, it was so exciting, so very different from a life of poverty in the back streets of Sicily. I made the most of my chance in that film—I grabbed fortune by the tail, like a big juicy prawn, and I gobbled it.'

Moments of silence were ticked away by a lovely old clock under a glass dome while La Neri dwelt on those early days of her career, which once it took off had been brilliantly successful. It wasn't only her beauty which had captured the imagination of the public, but she had possessed a warmth and a temperament that had reached out from the cinema screen and made the filmgoers love her.

'Have you brothers—sisters?' she asked Donna. 'Your father and I used to talk mainly of the films and I cannot remember if he had more than one child.'

'There was only me,' said Donna, with a tinge of regret. 'I'd have loved a sister, but Dad never remarried after my mother died, and devoted himself to his work.'

'It is good to have a sister,' Serafina agreed. 'And now, Donna, you will probably wish to see your apartment and to refresh yourself after your long journey. Did you travel by air to Rome?'

'No, I caught the Paris – Rome Express and travelled that way, through the Alps and all that lovely scenery.'

'What a hardy young creature you are! Those trains are usually packed like sardine cans—what then did you do in Rome?'

'I went to the Fountain of Trevi and threw in a coin,' Donna admitted with a smile. 'They say your wish gets granted if it's your first time in Rome.'

'Ah, so you also have a superstitious bone! I did the same, *cara,* the first time I was there —and my wish came true! What was yours, I wonder?' Serafina's smile was faintly mocking as her eyes swept Donna's face. 'Not to win a beauty contest, I think—perhaps to meet a man who would sweep you off your feet, eh?'

Donna refused to reply, for though she hadn't wished for a romantic involvement she had squeezed her eyes tight as she tossed the coin and hoped to find it pleasant and happy in Italy.

'*Roma, non basta una vita.*' Serafina spoke the words almost sensuously. 'The most fascinating city in the world, where happiness is to sit at a pavement table with a glass of *vino* and watch the people stroll by in all their differences. Did you stay long enough to see the sun set over the dome of St. Peter's?'

'I stayed a day and a night,' Donna said softly, remembering that sunset experience from her hotel balcony, the sky like a huge green lake as the flaming sun fell away and the stairway streets with their lines of laundry were lost in the dusk. She had eaten dinner at the hotel but had felt the urge to drink coffee on the *piazza* near the Bernini fountains. Then she had hired a *carrozza* and asked the driver to take her to the Colosseum, where the moonlight had been shining over that great auditorium where long ago the Christians had been torn by lions for the amusement of the Roman crowds.

Standing there among the ghosts she had suddenly heard the sound of footsteps, of someone approaching her with deliberation, and remembering the tales that it wasn't wise in a foreign city for a stranger to walk alone,

Donna had turned to hurry back to her carriage and had found herself confronted by a tall man wearing his coat like a cloak about his shoulders, with a face so darkly tanned that his eyes gleamed like onyx.

'What,' he had asked in grating English, 'brings a Saxon girl to such a place—does she hear the roar of the crowd again as the lions are released from their cages, great tawny creatures padding across the sand of the arena, manes bristling, snarling lips drawn back to expose the greedy teeth?'

Donna had been too startled to reply, too alarmed by him to realise for a moment or two that she had seen him before, at the hotel where she was staying overnight. He had been dining a few tables away from her own, and what had caught her attention was the small ring that he wore in his left earlobe, just below the bold darkness of his hair.

'Why would you come to a place such as this,' he had swept a lean, expressive hand around the Colosseum where everything was quiet except for the sound of *cigales* grating away in a nearby grove of cypress and ilex trees, 'unless you felt the pull of the past. Listen carefully and you might hear the roar of the lions as they pounce.'

Donna had felt an impulse to run away, up the steps to the safety of the *carrozza* where the driver waited for her, drowsing in the moonlight with his elderly horse, but something about the Italian stranger and his remarks held her there . . . something about his looks gripped her imagination and made her realise how unchanging was the truly Latin face. This man might have stepped from a canvas which had been painted in Renaissance days. He stood in silhouette against the moonlit sky, his features boldly defined and somehow ruthless, and despite a tinge of fear Donna couldn't help but feel fascinated by this dark stranger . . . a tingling sensation like electricity seemed to run through her body. He looked at her and there was a magnetic quality to his eyes above the hard-boned nose, the thrust of his cheek-bones and the brooding curve of his mouth.

'Yes, you have a sensitivity which makes you aware of the past.' His eyes held hers beneath the sardonic slant to his black brows. 'You were here just as I was, Saxon girl with your hair like ripe wheat let loose on your shoulders for the centurions to admire before the lions leapt to tear your slim white throat.'

Donna shivered at the image he evoked and it seemed as if anything might be possible on a night such as this one, with the moon casting shadows around the vast arena where the Christians had died for their belief in the teachings of Paul, who had come to pagan Rome to establish the church of the crucified Christ. 'And what were you?' she asked. 'One of the cruel Romans feasting your eyes on the slaughter of the innocent Christians?'

'I was a gladiator from the island of Sicily,' he replied. 'On the nights before a special bout of cruelty, when Caligula would be there to watch the spectacle, they gave the gladiators what you might call a rather special treat—a girl from among the captive virgins. That could have been the first time we met, eh?'

He smiled briefly and glanced around the great arena where such awful things had taken place in the past, and there was something about the hard gravity of his face that made him remarkable in a way Donna found very disturbing. Her eyes measured his imposing height and as the shifting moonlight played over him she thought she saw etched into his features a certain look of pain.

'Perhaps a modern young woman from England might deny that she believes in renaissance—the rebirth of the spirit.' A smile moved about in his dark eyes like a distant light. 'It might seem to you a profane belief, *signorina.'*

But anything could have been believable in this place where time had stood still, and there was something in his eyes that plucked at feelings deep within Donna that no stranger had the right to disturb. 'I've never really thought about it, *signore.'* Reacting to that twinge of alarm she gathered her coat about her and moved away from him and as she hastened up the steps to her carriage she felt afraid that he would follow her . . . a Latin wolf, she told

19

herself, with a unique line in *faire l' aimable*.

Back at the hotel she discovered that a dance was in progress and as she hovered in the doorway of the Domino Room someone handed her a silver mask and she noticed that all the couples on the dance floor were masked. Suddenly she longed to join them, for this was her one and only night in Rome, but she didn't have a partner and was turning away from the music and the hail of coloured prisms from the immense circling ball in the ceiling when a hand came to rest on her waist. 'Will you dance with me, *signorina?*' a deep, rather gravelly voice requested, some inches above her fair head.

Donna spun quickly around and found herself confronted by a tall man in a dark suit, and again she was attacked by a combined feeling of fear and shyness. He was wearing a black domino which added a kind of menace to his face and she recognised him instantly, but this time he wasn't going to permit her to get away from him so easily. His fingers caught her by the wrist and she felt the strength in them. 'Come, you may not know the music they are playing, but they play it tonight in memory of a certain famous Italian who long ago went to America and became the embodiment of every woman's secret dream.'

The lean fingers took hold of the silver mask and Donna found herself submitting to the dark stranger as he adjusted the mask over her face. Through the slits she looked at him, but she didn't tell him that she did know what the music was called. Without a word she let him lead her on to the dance floor and there she entered his arms to the romantic strains of *Dream Lover*.

Donna danced with the dark stranger until the ballroom was empty and the orchestra packed up. They wandered out on to the terrace and they talked . . . he knew so much about Italy and she listened to him in a kind of dream. They didn't exchange names, but before they parted he asked her to take breakfast with him the following morning. He kissed her hand and thanked her for her company.

But he wasn't in the dining-room the following morning and there on her table was a single white rose and a note in a sealed envelope. *'In Italy we say che sera, sera. Perhaps one day we may dance together again, perhaps without our masks.'*

The note had been unsigned, and the rose had been pure white, just opening from a bud, and with a stem that was quite thornless. Donna knew what it symbolised to the tall Italian who had come into her life so strangely, and then departed without saying a real goodbye.

'And what did you think of Rome?'

Donna gave Serafina a startled look. 'Oh—I

thought it beautiful—*dolce*, and also just a little sad.'

'You are your father's daughter,' the actress said, with a smile. 'And now go with Enrico and he will show you to your apartment. We dine at eight o'clock.'

As Donna followed the footman up a flight of stairs enclosed by delicate iron handrails she wondered if Serafina's son lived here at the villa. She had used the collective term, which seemed to indicate the presence of other people. Perhaps there were guests staying here, Latins who took siesta in the afternoons, unlike English house guests who played tennis in the sunshine, or swam in the pool if their hostess had one.

When the door of her apartment closed behind Enrico's uniformed back, Donna kicked off her shoes and paddled her toes in the thick wool rugs that lay about on the floor of fine-grained wood. The furniture was in dark polished rattan, even to the bedhead. Curtains and covers were in Italian patterns, and there were brass oil-lamps in place of electricity. Never before had Donna worked in such attractive surroundings, and she felt a mounting sense of excitement.

She gazed at the wild mountain scenery from her balcony . . . this was Serafina's stronghold where she ruled like a princess and even had a bodyguard to ensure that she came to no harm. A fantastic person, whose memoirs promised to be as fascinating as she was.

Donna's heart beat fast and she felt certain she was going to enjoy working in Italy, which had welcomed her with such a strange encounter on the steps of the Colosseum. She pressed a hand to her throat and felt the pulse beating there as she recalled the powerful Latin face and the night-dark eyes. She had never in her life before met a man who dared to wear a gold ring in his ear . . . in the revolving witchlight of the Domino Room it had looked like the wedding ring from a slim female finger, gleaming there in the shadow of the man's black hair.

Who was he, and would she ever see him again? The only thing she really knew about him was that he came from Sicily, island of the lemon-tree . . . and the vendetta.

Chapter Two

Donna met other members of the household that evening and it was as she guessed, there were several guests staying at the Villa Imperatore, who were drinking cocktails in the *salone* when Donna entered the room. They didn't take any particular notice of her, being absorbed in gossip about mutual friends, or enemies, and though Donna spoke a little Italian, she was a trifle lost among those to whom it was their natural language.

Then a young man strolled towards her and directly Donna met his eyes she knew him to be Serafina's son. Slanting, jade-green eyes set in a remarkably good-looking Latin face, which when he drew near was marked by lines which Donna suspected were caused by a love of pleasure rather than hard work. When he smiled at her those jade eyes crinkled in a way most women would find disturbingly attractive, but Donna's main reaction was one of curiosity. So this was the son Serafina had left with her husband while she had sought the adulation of the world, and now she was a woman of fame and wealth her son chose her company in preference to his father's.

Donna didn't return his smile but gave him a cool-eyed look. He knew she was his mother's secretary, and he probably assumed that part of her duties was to be nice to him.

His eyes flicked her up and down, taking in her dress of soft brown material, the neck-plunge outlined by silvery bands of silk. Her bosom beneath the dress hinted at where the silk cast silvery shadow, was girlishly young. Around her throat she wore a plaited band of silver, but no other adornment, and compared to the other women in the room she looked the image of simplicity.

'What beautiful hair you have.' He smiled beguilingly, as if never in his life had any girl resisted him for long. 'And what restful skin, as if it might be perfectly cool to touch.'

'Touch me, Signor Neri, and I'll slap your face,' she rejoined, 'and probably lose myself a very good job.'

'Ah, a girl of spirit and fire despite the cool blonde looks.' He stroked a finger down his cheeks as if warning her that one day he would touch her in the same way and she wouldn't slap his face. 'What would you like to drink, Miss Lovelace? I suppose I must be formal until you permit that we become friends?'

'You Italian men are very sure of your-selves, aren't you?' she said, remembering that other Italian with his remarks she couldn't seem to put out of her mind. 'It must have something to do with your upbringing and the way your female relatives make little gods of you.'

'Don't you believe in making a fuss of little boys—and big ones?' he murmured. 'The pleasure isn't all one-sided, *signorina.*'

'Where I come from, *signore,* the boys and girls are treated equally. Boys aren't brought up to believe that girls love them on sight and are then prepared to be their devoted slaves.'

'Ah, don't you believe that it's possible to fall in love at first sight?' Something leapt into his eyes, a little gleam of challenge that made them brilliantly green. *'Intrigante!* Usu-ally the English girl who comes to Italy is searching for the passionate romance she has been unable to find in her own cool country.'

'I came to Italy to work,' Donna said, in a cool voice. 'And I would like a drink, if you were about to give me one. An orange blos-som.'

'You see, *signorina,* you are a romantic at heart.' He smiled as if he were quite certain that he would soon have her eating out of his hand. 'Every other woman in this room is drinking Campari or vodka, but you ask for an orange blossom—what exactly are the ingredients?'

26

'Gin and orange juice.' Donna's sense of humour wouldn't be denied and she gave a sudden laugh, warm and throaty. 'What did you imagine, *signore,* that it was made from crushed blossoms with a dash of rice wine? Nothing so exotic. As I told you, I'm just an efficient secretary who rather enjoys her work.'

'I wonder?' His jade eyes slid over her face and hair, combed back casually from her face and looped into a barrette. 'Water is sometimes still because it hasn't yet been disturbed, and you may find that our southern atmosphere will melt the icicles around your heart. I will fetch your drink and you will stay right here, eh?'

'You couldn't make me run away, *signore.*' Her smile was faintly teasing. 'You don't frighten me enough.'

His eyes narrowed when she said that, and then with Latin grace he sauntered to the drinks cabinet, made too confident by his many conquests, Donna reflected, to be shaken for more than a moment by a mere secretary. He was attractive and he knew it, but Donna had no intention of jeopardising this job by flirting with him. Serafina was the type of woman to be possessive of her belongings, and it certainly wouldn't please her to have her son paying attention to someone in her employment.

Donna glanced around the room and

supposed that Serafina was waiting for her guests to assemble before she made a grand entrance in a spectacular gown, looking a hundred times more attractive than anyone else.

And it was at that precise moment that La Neri did make her entrance into the *salone,* wearing a dress patterned in different shades of silver, magical as she moved, a pendant of diamonds burning like flames against her velvety skin, with matching eardrops and bracelets. A sigh of admiration swept around the room . . . but Donna caught her breath for a very different reason.

A man followed Serafina into the *salone,* clad in a dark dinner suit with a dress shirt in a deep wine colour instead of the traditional white. Donna knew his strong bone-structure immediately, that erect posture, that radiation of authority, that stillness in contrast to La Neri's physical radiance.

A look of shock sprang into Donna's eyes and she felt again the same reaction she had felt on the steps of the Colosseum, a desperate urge to run away before the man looked at her. She gave a nervous start when a cool glass was placed in her hand and she heard a voice murmur: 'Her beauty always takes my breath away and I'm her son. When I look at her I find it hard to associate her with down-to-earth passions, and yet I am the living proof that she has felt them. The orange blossom is to your taste?'

Donna had taken a deep gulp because her throat had gone so dry. Upon leaving Rome she had thought never to see again the dark stranger who had spoken to her so evocatively, yet he was here at the villa, and she felt again that disturbing thrill of the nerves to see shining against his black hair that small ring of gold.

'Who is he?' Donna couldn't hold back the words, and she could feel her heart beating fast as he stood just inside the room, slowly casting his dark eyes over the faces of the home guests who were gathered in small groups, talking together in the animated way of Italians. Soon his eyes would settle on her and there would be no escape from those feelings he had stirred to life that night in Rome.

'That's Lordetti,' she was informed. 'Rick Lordetti, probably the most envied man in Italy because he takes care of Serafina, who relies on him as on no other man, not even her broker or her priest. He's my mother's bodyguard.'

'You mean—he lives here at the Villa Imperatore?'

'Of course, though for the past week he has been in Rome on some personal business and during that time the villa has been more than ever like a fortress. When Rick is here to safeguard her, Serafina feels less nervous.' Her son gave a curt little laugh. 'She refuses to

29

believe that she's safe with anyone but Rick. She is amused by the idea that her son could protect her, but then her own son isn't a trained assassin.'

'Is that what he is?' And as Donna spoke those night-dark eyes were suddenly upon her face, but the look of recognition she had expected had become a glance of supreme indifference; he merely flicked her features and moved his gaze to someone else.

'Yes, that is what he is—my mother's hired henchman.'

Donna caught her breath sharply, and instantly jade-green eyes were looking down at her, as attentive as those other eyes had been dismissive. 'You have gone quite white, Miss Lovelace! But you don't have to let Lordetti bother you. You can ignore him. He dines with us because my mother feels easier if she has him nearby—she has a morbid fear of being abducted, of falling into hands that would abuse her, and she trusts no one as fully as she does her own highly paid Sicilian *guarda bravo*. Some months ago he took a stiletto in the ribs on her behalf and the steel broke in him. Must have been painful as hell, but he drove her car round those mountain bends at a speed beyond belief and saved her from the clutches of a motor-cycle gang. I doubt if the man has any interest in any woman but Serafina.'

Donna's fingers clenched around the glass

that held her drink . . . yes, she had known that night in Rome that he was a man with a sinister side to him . . . a man outside society but accepted as a close associate of one of society's most celebrated women. A man who lived dangerously but whose code of loyalty would be cast-iron.

'Strange,' drawled Serafina's son, 'the attraction of the hoodlum for the lady.'

'Surely you must feel grateful to him for saving your mother from a gang of kidnappers?' Donna glanced at the man beside her and saw that he was glowering across the room at Rick Lordetti, who seemed indifferent to everyone in the room except the elegant woman in the silvery gown, who turned to say something to him to which he responded with a brief, almost grave smile. Although Serafina wore high heels and was quite tall for a woman, Lordetti towered over her, unusually tall for a Latin male, with broad muscular shoulders under the smooth dark material of his single-breasted jacket.

'He's well paid for what he does, and for the risks he takes.' The look on the good-looking face of La Neri's son was frankly jealous, and there was a flare to his nostrils. 'But I'd kill him if I ever thought the rumours were true!'

'What—rumours?' Donna felt compelled to ask . . . to know.

'That he's Serafina's lover!'

They went in to dinner after that, being seated at a long beautifully set table in a dining-room furnished with antiques that must have cost a fortune. Great candlelit chandeliers shone over the table with its costly lace, crystal and silverware; its wine and flowers, and the Latin faces that made Donna seem very fair-skinned and alien, a pale sheen to her hair whenever she turned to the dark young man at her side.

His name was Adone Neri and she couldn't help thinking how well it suited him, but she had to be careful not to be too responsive, for once or twice Serafina had glanced down the table when her son laughed and her eyes had the hard glitter of emeralds.

But most of all Donna was aware of the man seated beside Serafina. He joined rarely in the vivacious conversation of her guests, quietly eating his food and no doubt on duty the whole time, vigilant of the woman who apparently made him forget all other women when he was in her presence. His eyes seemed to look right through Donna, and she felt hurt as well as indignant, for he had said such disturbing things in those hours they had danced together. The charm she remembered so vividly had become a cold indifference, and Donna wanted to hate him for looking at her as if he had never held her in his arms to the strains of romantic music . . . as if he had put that rose between the covers of a favourite book!

Telling herself she'd destroy the flower later that night, Donna wondered if Serafina was aware that when in Rome her faithful body-guard did as the Romans and flirted with other women. Here at the villa other women were obviously beneath his notice . . . or was it possible that La Neri was jealous and he didn't dare to openly recognise her secretary? Donna had heard that in her days as a great star Serafina had not only made her rivals weep but in a couple of instances had ruined their careers.

Donna glanced away from that dark indifferent face and though she wanted to believe her self-made explanation, she could see for herself that Serafina would always find men to bind to her remarkable beauty; men who would love her ruthlessness as well as her charisma.

The food was deliciously cooked and served, but Donna barely tasted it. She made bright conversation with Adone Neri, but all the time she was racked by a tormenting question. Was Rick Lordetti the lover of Serafina?

She gave a start when someone leaned across the table and addressed her in a supercilious voice. 'Are you in films, *bionda bella,* or do you act in commercials for television?'

The man had a manner that matched his voice and was clad in a velvet dinner jacket with a bow tie against a pale pink shirt. Donna gave him a direct look and said clearly: 'I am here to assist Signora Neri with the writing of her memoirs. I thought everyone knew I was her secretary.'

'A secretary, eh?' The man laughed and looked around him. 'How democratic of our hostess to invite members of her staff to the dinner table! It must have something to do with the red influence on our politics these days, or do you suppose the Mafiosi are involved?'

A few of those seated near the man broke into laughter, but at the end of the table a dark head was suddenly turned in his direction and Donna felt a cold little thrill as those night-dark eyes seemed to strip the skin from the foppish face that even looked as if it had been powdered. Not a word was said, but Donna saw the ringed, effeminate hand crumple the embroidered napkin, reach for a wine glass and the next instant send it toppling so its contents spilled on the lace cloth. A servant was quickly there to remedy the matter, to mop the wine, replace the glass and set the table in order again.

From beneath the shield of her dark lashes Donna watched as Serafina leaned a little towards Rick Lordetti and whispered something. His lips moved in a brief sardonic smile and Donna knew instantly that La Neri wouldn't hesitate to throw every single guest out of her villa if the mood took her, but the man beside her was a permanent fixture. He was everything to her, and those she invited to the Villa Imperatore to amuse her were puppets she might flick aside with her painted fingertips.

She glanced down the table at the flustered fop in the pink shirt and smilingly drawled. 'My dear Conte, do be careful what you say in front of Rick. His grandmother was a Sicilian witch, you know, and she taught him some of her tricks. I would also advise you not to mention the Mafia in his presence . . . he and they are sworn enemies and he might break your neck if he thought you had the idea he was part of their notorious organisation. Rick, my dear Carlo, is the only gentleman I have ever met in a very varied life.'

A flush mottled the Conte's face and there was a tremor to his self-indulgent mouth. So that, thought Donna, was one of the noblemen of Italy. It was no wonder La Neri preferred a Sicilian gunman at her side as a sort of uncrowned escort. They matched like the profiles on a bronze coin dug from ruins, and a little shiver ran through Donna as she saw the silvered fingertips slide across the back of Lordetti's right hand. 'Mine!' the gesture seemed to indicate. 'My castellan!'

Big bowls of fruit salad were brought to the table along with a luscious thick cream which most of the women declined. Donna was not among them, and she heard Adone laugh as she dipped her spoon and ate cream and fruit with frank enjoyment.

'How refreshing,' he remarked, 'to see a woman who is unafraid to enjoy her food.'

'Haven't you heard,' she smiled, 'secretaries sometimes go hungry when jobs are thin on the ground and the rent has to be paid? I love cream, anyway, and this is gorgeous!'

'From our own cows,' he said. 'My mother has a farm in the valley and I must take you down there one day and show you the live-stock. Do you ride—Donna?'

It hadn't taken him long to get around to her first name, but there seemed very little Donna could do about it. He had his mother's charm, and didn't seem to realise that he might lose her this job if he became too attentive.

'I am here to work,' she reminded him, 'I'm not one of your mother's house guests, and you should realise that she won't approve of a—a friendship between us. In a way I agree with that awful Conte across the table— I should eat with the rest of the staff and not get any ideas above my station.'

'Then who would I talk to at dinner?' he asked woefully. 'Some of these bored married women who are looking for a gigolo?'

'So long as you don't get the idea I'm looking for one,' Donna rejoined. 'Please, don't pay me too much attention or you'll get me dismissed from a job I rather want. I've never worked in Italy before, least of all for someone like your mother. I realise she's temperamental, but that's what makes her exciting, and already she's beginning to wonder if I'm flirting with you, *signore.*'

'Aren't you flirting with me, *signorina?*' he asked. 'I rather hoped you were—ah, how the eyes flash and suddenly have a tawny look! If Serafina hoped to keep me in my place, then she should have hired a secretary with scraggy hair and spots. Your skin is like that cream you have just eaten.'

When he leaned close to her as if he'd like to brush her skin with his lips, Donna drew quickly away, shaking her head at him and darting a look towards the head of the table . . . instantly her heart felt as if it jarred itself against her ribs, for she had caught a pair of dark eyes upon her, watching her intently from under brows that cast shadows on the lean, commanding face. So Rick Lordetti hadn't forgotten her, and she sat there with bated breath as the lid of his left eye slowly drooped in a wink of sardonic conspiracy.

Her breath caught in her throat. Was that what he wanted, a secret friendship with the new secretary, whom he wasn't prepared to recognise in front of his mistress!

Donna felt indignant and disillusioned, and she gave him in return a look of scorn which didn't seem to affect him visibly. He merely leaned back in his chair and the edge of his lip twitched as if with amusement. When Serafina turned from her other neighbour to say something to him, his entire attention was hers once more.

To the devil with him, Donna fumed inwardly. How dared he assume that behind Serafina's back a wink was as good as a nod to her secretary! And with a sudden air of recklessness she turned to Adone, and for the remainder of the evening she responded to his overtures and was careless of Serafina's disapproval.

In the *salotto grande* the rugs were taken from the parquet floor, the big stereo deck was piled with records and most of the guests danced until past midnight. In her reckless mood Donna quite enjoyed herself, and she didn't only dance with Adone but was approached by some of the other men, who bowed to her when they requested a dance but held her a little too close to well-tailored dinner suits as they circled the floor to the kind of music which had been popular during La Neri's reign in Hollywood.

It was the kind of music Donna had enjoyed once before, until there came a moment when one of her partners attempted to kiss her on the neck and she felt obliged to stamp on his foot in order to put a brake on his unwanted ardour.

There was a slight tussle and then he released her with a curse and she whirled away from him and slipped through the long open windows on to the *terrazza* outside, softly shadowed at one end and cool after the scented warmth of the *salotto*.

Donna realised that she was slightly exhausted by the dancing and her attempts to understand the conversation of her partners who didn't speak English. It felt good to be alone for a while and she stood by the stone parapet and took several deep breaths of the night air, which was faintly haunted by a night-flowering shrub that hung its starry flowers over the wall.

It took a few minutes for her to realise that another scent had joined that of the shrub . . . the drifting aroma of a strong but not unpleasant tobacco.

She cast a look behind her, to the left where the shadows were almost black and she faintly discerned a tall shape and the orange glow of a cigarette as it was drawn upon. Her pulses quickened. Her treacherous senses responded to that shape because it was taller than other men at the party. Oh lord, she would have to come out here just as that man had chosen to come and smoke a quiet cigarette! He'd think she was pursuing him when all the time she wanted to avoid him!

'Don't run away,' he drawled, and her fingers clenched the stone parapet as she heard again that gravelly voice that gave his words a kind of fateful significance. 'Just stay where you are and let me tell you that it's wiser if we pretend we've never met before. You need a well-paid job here on the Saracen coast, and why shouldn't you have it, but it's better if we remain strangers in front of Serafina.'

'Why, wouldn't your mistress approve?' Donna asked coldly. 'Doesn't she know that you try and pick up strange girls when you're in Rome and affected by the attitude of *dolce far niente?*'

'As I told you then, Donna *mia,* there is no strangeness between us. You felt the chemistry just as I did, and that kind of alchemy is a thing from the past. I didn't follow you from the hotel. I went to the arena quite independently and you were there, as if you had to go there, to meet me again.'

'Oh, stop it!' Donna turned in his direction, a sudden look of torment on her face. 'You frighten me, do you know that? I know you carry a gun and what you're paid to do with it, so don't tell me I've ever met anyone like you before. You're not the kind of—of friend I'd ever want!'

'Keep saying it often enough, sweetheart, and you might grow to believe it,' he said, in that grating voice of a man who probably smoked too much and accepted the danger with irony. 'Human beings always suppose they can set aside their feelings like a stale sandwich or a drink that's lost its fizz, but feelings are flesh and it's like trying to tear out a piece of yourself when you try not to care for someone.'

'Care?' she exclaimed. 'Are you having the gall to say I—I care for you? You're the last man on earth—a hired gunman!'

'I'm human like everyone else,' he drawled. 'I get those nights when I'd like nothing better than to lay my head on a loving shoulder.'

'With your gun under the pillow?'

'It was a sword in the old days.'

'Is that what you imagine you are—a kind of black knight for La Neri?'

'Sounds romantic, doesn't it?'

'Sounds nicer than hoodlum! Were you ever in Chicago, *signore?* You have a slight twang in your voice and I can't help being curious.'

'Women are curious creatures. Yes, I met Serafina in the States, only it was at Las Vegas, in one of the night clubs.'

'Were you the club's strong-arm man?'

'You—little devil!' He made as if to move in her direction, and then slid back into the shadows as they both caught the sound of someone approaching. Rick Lordetti was a barely discernible shape again when Adone Neri reached Donna's side. 'There you are,' he said. 'I'm glad you didn't slip away to bed without saying goodnight to me. What a night, *carina!* The moon is softly dying among the stars.'

Donna, still inwardly shaken by what Rick Lordetti had said to her, and still very much aware that he was within earshot of what Adone was saying, caught at the young man's arm and gave him a beseeching look. 'I am tired—it's been a long day and I'm going indoors now——'

'When you've kissed me goodnight.' He caught hold of her and pulled her against him. 'I don't have to make you, do I? You aren't that kind of a girl?'

'I'm not the kind of a girl who goes around kissing every man I meet,' she said, trying to pull away from him. But now he had his arms around her Adone wasn't going to let her go easily and his eyes were gleaming as he brought his face down towards hers——

'Let the lady go,' drawled a voice from the shadows. 'Can't you see you're annoying her?'

Adone swung round in Rick Lordetti's direction. 'Who's that?' he demanded.

Rick moved forward and a faint ray of moonlight fell across his lean dark face. His teeth were bared in a slightly dangerous smile.

'You!' Adone quivered as if a whip had flicked his skin. 'Up to your usual tricks of skulking and spying, Lordetti? Well, don't try that stuff on me! Let me tell you, if I had my way you wouldn't come within a hundred miles of my mother, let alone walk in and out of her rooms as if you have rights. You're just a thug she overpays for the privilege!'

'You pompous little cockerel.' A match was struck and the flame flared at the tip of a cigarette, casting its brief light over Rick's inscrutable face. Smoke jetted from his nostrils as his eyes flicked Adone's enraged face. 'When did you ever earn a wage, one way or another? I'd say you were very much privileged yourself, but not to the extent of forcing your attentions on Miss Lovelace, who will most certainly earn her keep.'

'Damn you!' Adone flushed deeply. 'I could knock your head off—you, Lordetti, you're nothing but a gigolo!'

Rick drew on his cigarette until the tip glowed hotly, then he leaned forward and snapped his fingers in Adone's face. 'You're like a turn out of the Commedia Dell 'Arte, *mio*. Miss Lovelace will assume that Italians are all steam and no broth, so why not simmer down before you get your pretty face reorganised into something not quite so fetching.'

'Blast you!' Adone was fuming, and when he swung a punch Rick adroitly stepped to one side and clipped the younger man across the nose. This had the instant effect of making it bleed, and grabbing the handkerchief out of his pocket Adone clamped the cambric to the offended feature and looked at Rick Lordetti as if he'd like to kill him. 'You won't get away with this,' he mumbled. 'I'll see to it that Serafina fires you!'

'Yes, you see to it,' Rick drawled. He turned casually to Donna, who had watched the dispute with a mixture of fright and fascination. She couldn't feel entirely sorry for Adone, for he was obviously an indulged young man who liked his own way, but what had given her a shocking little thrill was the feeling that Rick Lordetti had been defending her . . . that he had not been able to stand by while Adone pestered her.

'Shall we go in?' Rick stood looking at her and she nodded and walked along the *terrazza* with him, while Adone stood mopping his nose. When she glanced back, Rick gave a gravelly laugh. 'A little blood-letting will cool him down, so don't be too concerned. You didn't wish to be mauled by him, did you?'

'Of course not!' She glanced up at the tall Sicilian and realised anew how much power there was in the broad shoulders; he could probably make mincement of someone like Adone even though he was considerably older. 'Thanks for stepping in, but aren't you worried that he'll make trouble between you and his mother?'

'Not in the least.' Rick studied her face as they paused by the lighted glass doors of the *salotto*. 'There is very little trouble the young man can make between Serafina and me. He isn't the one who represents any problem.'

'You mean——' Donna was caught, held by his dark eyes, 'it would take another woman to do that?'

'Exactly.'

Sometimes it took only a single word to say everything, and Donna felt her heart strangely gripped as she looked at Rick Lordetti, just faintly smiling, the cigarette drooping from his lip. He was tough, and he could probably be very rough, but somewhere deep inside him Donna knew there was a tenderness that melted her very insides. She swayed a little and he caught at her wrist, holding it tightly yet very gently. 'I—I never thought I'd see you again,' she whispered.

'I knew I'd see you.' His thumb moved against the soft inner skin of her wrist. 'I looked in the hotel register and saw your name—Lovelace. I knew a girl with that name was on her way to the villa to work for Serafina.'

'Perhaps I should go away—I've already caused trouble between you and Adone.'

'Life is a troubled thing, and there's no running away from life.'

Donna's pulse was pounding under his touch and he knew it—oh God, there was no sense to this! It was beyond reason that she could feel so disturbed by a man she barely knew . . . a man who didn't deny that Serafina had a prior claim on him.

'I—I must have had too much wine,' she gasped, pulling away from him. 'Too much of everything for one day—tomorrow I'll smile at it all and see it for what it is.'

'What is it, *belladonna?*'

'The fascination of the devil! You're different, that's all, and I've only known college boys and a comedian who thought he was irresistible when he was only a tiresome bore. Tomorrow I'll be the same again!'

'Yes, everything seems more ordinary in the daytime.' Rick drew away from her and gave a sardonic bow. 'The only problem is that when night falls and the stars take shape again, we are inclined to forget our resolutions. *Buona notte, signorina.*'

'Goodnight, *signore.*'

Donna fled away from him yet again . . . taking with her the troubling awareness that they would meet tomorrow and by daylight he would still affect her more potently than anyone else she had ever met.

Chapter Three

In the days that followed Donna was kept busily at work in the most charming office she had ever worked in, at a Renaissance desk on which the pale-green Hermes typewriter looked very modern and out of place. Overhead the ceiling was painted to represent a goddess with her retinue of maidens clad in flowing draperies that revealed curvaceous arms and legs. The group idled on the banks of a stream in which they were reflected as if in a mirror.

The walls of the room were panelled in rich dark wood and across the floor was spread a lovely old carpet. Beyond the long windows stood a Judas tree aflame with deep-red flowers—blood of the traitor. But what fascinated Donna and made her gaze across the small courtyard was the black stone knight that stood sentinel there, head slightly bowed, hands in gauntlets crossed upon the hilt of a sword.

The very first time Donna noticed the

figure, she felt her heart give a leap and recalled what she had said to the man who was Serafina's bodyguard. 'Are you a sort of black knight for La Neri?'

It was a romantic idea, Donna realised. Probably an attempt on her part to soften the harsh reality of what he really was, a man hired to protect a rich woman, swift and deadly with the gun he carried, and in many ways outside the law. How many years, Donna wondered, had he lived such a life? How long would it take before he became completely armoured against people, that inner core of warmth no longer able to leap into life . . . as she had seen it, felt it, that night on the *terrazza?*

Since that night he had kept at a cool distance, never betraying by a flicker of an eyelid in Serafina's presence that he had the remotest interest in her secretary. Donna didn't know whether to feel relieved or rather piqued, for there had been something dangerously exciting in having a man leap to her defence . . . a man who was far from being an impetuous boy. It had been something of a revelation of what life must have been like long ago when men had been prepared to duel over the honour of a woman.

Anyway, she was truly relieved that Adone's threats had come to nothing, and if Serafina knew of the fracas she certainly didn't know the cause, for Donna felt sure she would have been told to pack her bags and leave the villa. Adone, in fact, must have been quite intoxicated, for he seemed vague about some of the details of the incident and actually asked Donna if he had annoyed her in any way. She thought it wise to say he hadn't, and he rumpled his hair and gave her a quizzical look. 'An Italian should always drink wine,' he said. 'He'll sing on wine but turn nasty on whisky. I suppose I must have said something Lordetti didn't like, because I remember him giving me a karate chop across the nose. I don't tangle with him when I'm sober—he's dangerous because he never loses his temper, and he never takes more than one drink. It is the danger in him that Serafina likes.'

Adone leaned over the desk where Donna was sitting, and where she had been working busily until the son of the house had come strolling into the room.

'How very neat,' he murmured, but his eyes dwelt only briefly on the typed page and were now upon her cyclamen pink shirt with its open collar showing the slim gold chain and crucifix around her neck. 'But what a shame for a girl to be shut up with a typewriter when the world outside is such a pleasant place, and there is a *trattoria* down on the coast where we could eat huge roasted prawns and a *lasagne* that would melt your heart. Come and lunch with me, eh?'

Donna firmly shook her head, well aware

that once he got her down on the coast in his very fast car the lunch hour would stretch into the afternoon and instead of a neat pile of typing on thick creamy paper, Serafina's dictation would still be on the recorder and she would want to know if her secretary had been having a sleep instead of getting on with her work.

'Your mother's a generous employer,' she told Adone, 'and I like my work. She has remarkable recall, you know. She remembers events in the past as if they had happened yesterday.'

He shrugged and began to prowl about the room, a frown joining his dark brows together. He wore tailored slacks and a rough-silk shirt, and with his rumpled hair was very attractive. It was a pity, Donna told herself, that Serafina had never insisted that he work for his living, for he was idling his life away in meaningless affairs with women, and dulling his sense of boredom with the whisky that didn't suit his liver or his temperament.

'Don't you ever get the urge to do a job of work?' Donna asked him. 'Doesn't it worry you to waste your energy and health on a monotonous round of pleasures that must leave you with hangovers of the spirit as well as the body?'

He lounged against the rococo carving of a bookcase, and looked at once a little too wise and worn for his age, and yet had that air

50

of the spoiled rich boy. 'Encouraging sign,' he murmured, 'when a girl wants to save a man from himself. What sort of occupation would you suggest I take up?'

'You play an excellent game of tennis,' she said, 'so why not teach other people to play?'

'Keep the body occupied and fit at the same time, eh?' His lips curved into a smile. 'I believe you're a little Puritan, and I see you wear a crucifix. Are you out to save my soul before it gets scorched in the fires of hell?'

'I'm being serious,' she said. 'A man in your position could start a really good sports club—tennis, squash, badminton. When you have skills they should be put to use, but of course if you prefer to fritter your life away that's your business, *signore.*'

The faintly mocking smile died out of his green eyes as he studied her behind the antique desk, wheaten hair drawn back from her brow, and perched on her nose the horn-rimmed spectacles she needed when at work. They gave her a slightly prim and proper air, and suddenly Adone was giving her what could only be called a melting Italian look.

'I could put you between warm slices of bread and eat you!' he exclaimed, and in one impetuous stride he was beside her, with a flick of his hands he had removed her glasses, and in a lithe bend of his body he had placed a kiss on her mouth.

'Adorable, maddening Miss Prim,' he

exulted. 'You are right, my life was a waste-land before you came into it and it is time I settled down. Will you be my wife?'

Donna gave a laugh and retrieved her glasses from his hand. 'You'd die of shock if I said *grazie,* let's go and see the priest right away.'

'I would be enchanted.' He touched the little gold cross that rested in the hollow of her throat. 'A girl who loves for life, eh? Are you afraid Adone would make a restless hus-band who would soon be chasing after other women?'

'Old habits die hard.' For some fleeting reason she thought of Rick Lordetti and her eyes sobered. 'You shouldn't be in here, *signore,* talking such nonsense and interrupting my work. Your mother would be displeased if she came in and found me wasting my time with you instead of typing this chapter. She'll want to check it over later today.'

'If you married me, Donna, you would never have to work again.'

'Really?' she murmured. 'Would your mother keep both of us in idle luxury?'

'*Carina,* you are cruel! I thought your heart as soft as your skin.' His green eyes dwelt on her young figure. 'How I would relish the right to make you faint with desire—you are very desirable, do you realise that?'

'Please stop it!' Donna spoke with a sudden nervous sharpness. 'You are bored and have nothing better to do than to come in here saying foolish things—now look what you've made me do!' She had run some words together that would make an awful mess of the carbon copies if she tried to erase them and giving Adone an annoyed look she tore the sheets out of the typewriter. 'Please go away!'

'On one condition.' He lounged there tinkering with the antique inkstand adorned with brass nymphs.

'I refuse to make conditions in order to get a little peace, *signore.*'

'Then I remain and there will be no *tranquillita* for you.'

'You really are a spoiled brat,' Donna informed him. 'You should have had my father in charge of you—he'd have seen to it that you got a little more discipline.'

'Ah, but can I help it if I find you *simpatica* and feel the need to be with you?' Adone roved her slightly flushed face with his jade eyes and a tiny nerve flickered in his lip. 'Say you will dine with me this evening and then I'll leave you to rattle away at the scandalous memoirs.'

'They aren't scandalous.'

'Give them time, *carina,* they will be as soon as Serafina starts to talk about the film world. My beautiful, glittering mother has a star's need to be in the public gaze and to be at the same time untouchable—she wants her book to be a best-seller, and in this day and age that is only achieved on the grand scale if there is a layer of ham, butter and spice between the covers. Dear Miss Prim, I hope you are prepared to be shocked when La Neri starts to reveal a number of spicy secrets about the people with whom she has worked—secrets they will be unable to dispute, because she has a very surprising virtue—she never tells lies.'

'I'm not a prude, you know.' Donna wound fresh paper and carbon into the Hermes. 'I didn't come here expecting the memoirs of a famous film star to be like Peg's Paper. My father was part of the filmmaking world and I realise its racy aspects.'

'It is true, then, what the very famous Hitchcock says about the cool-looking blonde, that inside she is a smouldering flame?'

'I shall really start to smoulder, *signore,* if you don't go and amuse yourself somewhere else. I have work to do!'

'I said I would go away like a good boy if you agreed to dine with me tonight.' He leaned forward and touched a finger to the little cleft in her chin. 'Don't be obstinate. Give in to what you really want and say you will come.'

'Has no woman ever resisted you?' Donna asked, jerking away from his touch.

'Don't force me to be immodest, *cara.'* His green eyes crinkled into a smile that was suddenly beguiling. 'After a hard day's work what can be nicer for a girl than to put on a charming dress, to climb into a fast car and be driven to a good restaurant? Can you resist?'

Donna thought about it and realised that the invitation did sound attractive, but all the same she couldn't quite forget that Adone Neri was inclined to be amorous and she didn't want to wind up on one of those mountain curves fighting for her honour.

'Ask yourself which is the best of two evils,' he murmured. 'My mother finding me in here with you, or a cool drive in the mountains. In each there is an element of risk and it's for you, Donna, to take your choice.'

Donna glanced about the charming room in which she worked and out upon the sunlit courtyard where the figure of the stone knight caught and held her gaze. Suddenly she could have laughed at the idea of being afraid of Adone . . . suddenly all that mattered was that she remain at the Villa Imperatore.

'What time would you like me to be ready?' she asked, and when she glanced back at Serafina's son he merely seemed a good-looking Lothario who had never really harmed anyone.

'If you could be ready by seven-thirty that should give us plenty of time to be together.' His eyes gleamed pure green in that moment, holding Donna's a moment before he swung on his heel and strolled to the door, where he gave her a slight bow. *'Arrivederci, cara.'*

The door closed behind him and Donna proceeded with her work, pushing to the back of her mind any lingering doubts she might have regarding the wisdom of being dated by Adone Neri. On those mountain roads, she had to remember, there would be no dark-eyed knight to come to her rescue.

She smiled at the thought. How absurd of her to think of Rick Lordetti like that . . . he was probably far more dangerous than Adone could ever be. No woman in La Neri's position would employ as her bodyguard a man who wasn't capable of great ruthlessness in dealing with those who attempted to harm her . . . according to Adone he had already demonstrated his ability to snatch Serafina out of harm's way and in doing so had sustained a knife injury.

Something seemed to stab beneath Donna's own ribs . . . she was a naive fool if she really imagined that a man like Rick Lordetti had any real interest in her. Serafina was the woman in his life. La Neri, with her great beauty and fame; her sensuous eyes that dwelt on the dark Sicilian with the gleam of possession in them.

Donna switched on the tape-recorder and listened to Serafina relating incidents of her girlhood in Sicily, the kind of background Rick shared with her . . . two people who knew what it was like to grow up in a tough environment where poverty was shared by everyone and accepted with a kind of rough and ready courage. Those back streets, according to La Neri, had been forever hung with lines of washing, noisy at all times of the day with people shouting across to each other from rickety balconies that almost touched, teeming with ragged children whose big beautiful eyes were made luminous by constant hunger.

La Neri had used her beauty in order to get away from the noise, the hunger and dirty streets. Rick Lordetti had used his toughness and was a man who would know his way about in the jungles of big cities when darkness fell. His snarl would be as menacing as that of the other creatures who had prowled out of the mean streets in search of prey . . . or their own lost souls. He would often choose to be solitary, like the stone figure that stood in the sunshine that could never warm it.

Donna gave a little shiver and wished she could push him out of her thoughts as easily as she pushed out the handsome Adonis who had proposed marriage to her as if he were asking for a piece of candy.

But Rick Lordetti had never been a lotus eater like Adone . . . he was a man whom she felt to be branded with memories which had left irremovable scars. Some awful happening in his past had made him a hard man who gradually thrust all tender feeling deep into the darker recesses of himself, burying it out of sight until one day it would no longer exist and he would be like that figure out on the patio. He would have turned to stone and never again would tiny flames leap to life in the density of his Sicilian eyes, beckoning a girl to come and burn in them.

Donna drew a hand across her eyes as if to shut out that still stone figure. She must be affected by something in the Italian atmosphere . . . the man fascinated her because he was like no other man she had known. He was no knight in blemished armour, but merely a henchman who took care of a rich woman, in more ways than one! Adone had said he had the run of Serafina's rooms as if he had rights, and she'd have to be as innocent as a schoolgirl if she believed he went in and out of that luxurious bedroom in order to look under the bed!

It came as a relief when the door of the office opened and the footman appeared with Donna's mid-morning tray, on which stood a cup of coffee, home-baked flaky biscuits and cream cheese. There was also a big velvety peach with the leaf still attached. 'Oh, how nice!' she exclaimed.

'The *signore* sent it,' the footman told her, his eyes politely blank.

'The *signore*?' Her heart had leapt with a crazy, unimaginable hope.

'Signor Neri.'

'Please thank him for me.' She smiled, and was inwardly dismayed that her heart could behave like this when common sense told her that Adone was the one who would regard a girl as a peach; that he probably had an entire repertoire of charming gestures designed to weaken a girl's resistance.

Alone once more, she wandered with her coffee to the long glass doors and stood there looking at the stone knight through the leaves and dark-red flowers of the Judas tree. Donna had never thought of herself as a romantic, but since coming to Italy she had started behaving like one ... like some girl in a novel who felt herself drawn to a stranger for some inexplicable reason ... a dark stranger who had disturbed and fascinated her from the first moment she had looked into his eyes.

Was she so very wrong in believing there had been a certain wistfulness in those eyes? That they had dwelt on her as they owned her but could never have her?

Her throat suddenly ached and she quickly blinked away the tears that filled her eyes. 'Stop haunting me!' Unaware, she had moved across the patio and was standing in front of the black knight. But the head was bowed in the helmet of chain-metal, and the hands were stony still on the hilt of the sword. Only the birds had voice and wing ... the knight kept his silence and his vigil.

Donna cooled her skin with toilette perfume and dressed for the evening in a silk-jersey dress the colour of green grapes, finely pleated from the hips to the ankles, worn with a chenille jacket with black pearl buttons. The effect was soignée, for she had arranged her hair in a glossy knot at the nape of her neck and added black pearl studs to her earlobes.

A slight nervousness affected her and she could feel the pulse beating under the skin of her neck. Perhaps she should have been firm with Adone and taken a chance on his mother finding them alone in the office, yet all the same it felt nice to dress up for dinner at a restaurant, and she was pleased with the dress she was wearing for the first time.

Green girl, she thought, allowing these Latin men to impair the cool serenity she had been so proud of. Well, no one could say she didn't look cool on the outside, even if her heart was no longer sure of itself.

Then to her confusion Adone was waiting for her at the foot of the stairs, looking incredibly handsome in a white dinner jacket over dark slimline trousers, his poplin shirt blue and immaculate, a glint of sapphires at his cuffs.

'*Che bella!*' He planted a foot on the bottom step and watched her come down to him. He reached out a hand and took hold of hers, possessively. 'You are charming, *cara.* You are adorable!'

'You look rather nice yourself, Adone.'

'*Grazie.*' His eyes smiled into hers. 'That is how it should be, that two people should be a suitable match for each other. Just think how adorable will be our *bambini.*'

'Now don't start that again,' she protested, but he only laughed and drew her towards the *salone,* where he threw open the door and stood framed with Donna in the opening.

'We are just off,' he announced to the couple who occupied the room, the woman stretched out on the sofa with the soft lighting playing over her hair, the man tall and dark by the open windows, the inevitable cigarette between his lips. In an instant Donna was aware of him to the roots of her fair hair and she saw the thoughtful narrowing of his eyes as he drew on his cigarette and then flicked a look at Adone.

'Don't drive like a contestant for the next rally,' Serafina drawled at her son. 'Donna suits me admirably as a secretary and I don't wish to lose her. In fact I'm wondering if it's wise to let you have her for the evening— she's an amazingly unspoilt creature and I knew and liked her father, and I don't think he'd approve of you, *caro.*'

'I shall guard this girl, Serafina, as Rick guards you.' Adone shot a glance at the other man, who fractionally raised a black eyebrow and jetted smoke from his nostrils. 'Surely I couldn't take as a better example my own mother's cavalier?'

'Is that what you are, Rick?' Serafina slid her sensuous jade eyes to the tall figure of her bodyguard. Their eyes met and she laughed purringly, as if at a very personal joke between them. 'There are few men like Rick, and I wish you were like him, *caro,* but you have the warm, impetuous nature and it pleases me to spoil you because I saw too much hunger when I was a girl; too much longing for the sweet things of life. Enjoy your evening, Adone, and do try to behave yourself.'

'Of course, *madonnina.'* He moved blithely to the sofa and bent over to kiss Serafina, and Donna could hear the actress laughing amusedly as she reached up to caress the face that bore such a likeness to her own.

Then, feeling dark eyes upon her face, Donna gave in to the compulsion to look at the man whose body and soul Serafina seemed to hold on a chain. Why didn't they marry? Divorce was no longer impossible in Italy and Donna felt quite certain that Rick was La Neri's lover. How could any man spend hours in the company of a woman so seductive and not make love to her?

His eyes were still and dark as Donna met them, and then they slid over her slim figure in the graceful green dress and it was as if he ran a hand very lightly over her body. She reacted as if actually touched and her eyes flashed appeal and anger at him. 'Don't!' The cry was in her eyes. 'I don't want to know what Serafina feels when you take her in your arms!'

She gave a start when Adone took her by the arm. 'Come, it's time we were going.' His eyes caressed her face, but she felt nothing. She went with him from the room, but felt as if she left some vital part of herself behind. It was madness to feel attracted to a man who belonged to another woman . . . a possessive woman with a terrible temper, whose long fingernails would rip into her if she ever caught Rick actually touching her.

Donna felt sure he wanted to touch her . . . she had seen his eyes go curiously bleak when Adone had taken hold of her arm. A tremor ran through her which the young Italian must have felt for when they paused beside his sleek Maserati he gazed down at her with a kind of smouldering concern in his eyes. 'Don't be scared by Lordetti—I know you are, Donna. I noticed the way you looked at him, for you probably sense the kind of man he is. If you must have it straight out, he has killed in his time.'

'Oh no!' Her eyes pleaded that it not be true, but Adone nodded and his eyes were absolutely serious.

'It happened a long time ago in a dockside fight that ended in the death of Rick's opponent when he was knocked to the ground and struck his head against a stone bollard. The police arrested Rick and he was tried for manslaughter, and though he was never found guilty of the actual killing it was established that he started the fight and had a motive for wanting the man dead. It seemed he had been a member of the Mafioso and had been responsible for a tragedy in Rick's family.'

'A tragedy?' Her eyes searched Adone's in the wild hope that he could tell her what had happened. 'Do you know the details?'

'His mother was murdered.' Awful, unbelievable words. 'She was an American and something of a sculptress, who met and married a Sicilian while on a trip to the island. They had a small olive farm and when her husband died in what was called an accident she blamed his death on the Mafioso and said they had killed him because he refused to pay protection money to their organisation. Then one day she died herself for being outspoken about those terrible people, and Rick—he was only a youth at that time—swore he'd find the killer and have his vengeance. No one doubts that if the man hadn't died by hitting his head he would have died at Rick's hands.'

Adone paused, significantly. 'So you see, Donna, you aren't the only person to feel nervous of him. It's that banked-down ruthlessness that makes him perfect in my mother's eyes. Indispensable would be the polite word to describe what he is to her, and I doubt if she could live without him.'

Adone touched Donna's cold face. 'It is a shocking story, but it adds to Serafina's sense of security that Rick's reputation is a tough one. It makes him more formidable as a bodyguard—but you're in no danger from him, *cara*. In all the years I've known him he has never looked at any other woman but La Neri.'

'What about when he goes to Rome?' Donna spoke the words impulsively, unable to forget the way Rick had looked at her, those eyes of his holding tiny flames that might blaze up and consume her if she ever got close to him, when Serafina was not around.

Adone shrugged and opened the car door. 'Who knows? He has a partnership in a club there, but if he sees other women, and if Serafina knows of it, she never mentions it. To my certain knowledge her trust in him is implicit, and you have seen for yourself that he's entirely devoted to her. Other women could be but a passing diversion. Hereabouts there has never been the faintest whisper of any kind of infidelity. I have doubted myself if the man has a heart.'

Donna slid into her seat and moments later the Maserati was speeding away from the villa. She felt Adone's knee against her leg and heard him give a slight chuckle when she delicately withdrew from the contact.

'What I like about you,' he said, handling the racy car with expertise once they were on those serpentine bends that twisted and turned all the way to the coastline, 'is that you're rather like an elusive perfume that a man can't forget once he has breathed it. It amazes me that you are still single, and still very much the *vergine*. Have you ever fancied an English lover?'

'I wonder why it is,' she said, 'that foreigners always imagine that English women are so —forward? I daresay the majority of us behave just like Italian girls. We wait to fall in love before we start throwing our favours around.'

'Ah, that would be something, Donna, to have you throwing your favours at me.' He shot a glance at her just as they rounded a bend that seemed to hover in space above the rocks and the sea. Donna closed her eyes in horror, but a moment later they were still on the road, though the wheels seemed hardly to touch the tarmac.

'Why are Italians such reckless drivers?' she asked breathlessly.

'Perhaps to compensate for having to be cautious when we start courting a girl of virtue.'

'What is the object, Adone, to make me beg for mercy? If you'd slow down a little, then I might just enjoy this drive.'

'Chicken-hearted?' he mocked. 'Some women love a fast driver.'

'And I don't doubt you speak from

vast experience.'

'Does it worry you to be with a man who has frankly enjoyed the company of the opposite sex? Do you prefer the monkish type?'

'I enjoy good company, but I don't like men who show off.'

'You think I am showing off, *cara?*'

'I believe you may be trying to prove something, perhaps to yourself. A strong man doesn't have to flaunt his abilities.'

'You are saying I am not a strong man?'

'You're a spoiled one, Adone. You're handsome, secure in your mother's affection and her need to see you never want for anything. But you know in your heart that you're wasting your life in lots of ways. A woman never wholly respects a man who has achieved nothing but expertise behind the wheel of a fast car, and in the various boudoirs he has charmed his way into.'

'So you prefer Don Quixote to Don Juan?'

'Any time. To tilt at windmills even if you take a toss is better than never trying at all.'

'So what are you searching for, Donna, a knight who carries a sword? A foolish Quixote who puts honour before everything else? Do you really hope to find someone like that in this day and age? We live in a materialistic world, and ideals are very much out of fashion.'

'What a pity,' she murmured. 'It must have been quite something to have lived in an age when men were prepared to be honourable—like the men whose white stone monuments stretch across the old battlefields as far as the eye can see. My father once took me to see them, and I'll never forget the words carved on one of those headstones. Courage, they said, is the soul of man, and honour the shining sword that he carried. My father wanted me to know about sacrifice. He said it was a dying grace in the human race and that if ever I found it I was to pay it homage.'

'Ah, what a girl!' Adone laughed softly, almost incredulously. 'You are like a good deed in a naughty world, for with you it isn't just talk, is it? You truly believe that such things as chivalry and self-sacrifice still exist—*Cristo santo,* what I have to live up to, and I am such a late starter!'

Donna had to give way to a laugh. 'It would be nice, Adone, to meet Sir Lancelot, but I don't really expect to. As you say, we live in a world that puts too much emphasis on material possessions and getting ahead regardless of other people's feelings. I think the most awful type of man I can think of is the tycoon who tyrannises over everyone in his employ and builds himself images of gold to worship. Fancy any girl supposing that such a man could love her! It would be like loving Hitler!'

Adone laughed with delight. 'More and more you brighten my life, *carissma,* and to think I imagined that Serafina's secretary would be a blue-stocking with a severe haircut and a sharp tongue. What a delightful surprise when you arrived. I could hardly believe my luck!'

'I didn't come to the Villa Imperatore on your behalf,' she reminded him. 'Your mother doesn't really approve of our—friendship, you know.'

'She thinks I shall lead you astray.' The car swept into view of the harbour, where the sea lay still and shadowy under the stars until they drew nearer and the myriad sea-craft lights were reflected from the rigging of fishing boats and yachts. Some miles out there was a curving watch-tower above the slabs of rock, throwing its light in a circle.

'Is that your intention?' Donna asked, as they swept into the forecourt of a sea-front restaurant where music was playing, drifting out from lighted windows and stealing among flowering bushes of oleander and white clusters of magnolia. A charming, unexpected place, for Donna had felt sure that Adone's taste in restaurants was rather more sophisticated.

The throb of the car engine died to stillness and Adone sat looking at Donna in the glow of the dashboard, his face as detailed as that on a Roman coin, his eyes as slanting and green as a leopard's. 'I lie awake thinking about you,' he said frankly. 'I long to be with you—to hold you in my arms. I have never known a girl like you before—intelligent, with a mind of your own, and yet inno-cent——'

'Adone,' she broke in, with a touch of desperation, 'we've known each other such a short time and you're rushing me with your charm—oh yes, you have it and you know it. You're probably the best-looking man I've ever seen, but you live in a world of sophisti-cation and I just seem different from other women you've known and probably been half in love with. When the gilt wears off the gingerbread——'

'I don't think it will, in this instance.' His fingers touched her hair. 'Like silky wheat in the sun—there are so many things I should like to give you—myself most of all.'

'Please——' Donna knew that for some deep and inward reason she was tonight sus-ceptible to Adone's looks and the things he said, but caution was warning her that if she dared to show him that he was getting under her skin with his amorous and attractive charm she would have trouble with him. He was every inch the warm-blooded, impetuous Latin, and Donna didn't want to become part of an involvement that would never satisfy her deepest longings.

'I'm awfully hungry,' she said. 'Can't we go in and eat?'

'You sit so close to me but you are running

away from me,' Adone said, with unexpected perceptiveness. His hand reached for her face and he made her look at him. 'I have an ambition, Donna, and it is to melt away your English reserve and have you warm and yielding in my arms. You are lonely—as we are all lonely inside ourselves, and I have the advantage of knowing you find me—not distasteful, eh?'

He was remarkably handsome, there was no denying that. His looks and his Latin seductiveness were inherited from his mother, and in that moment Donna wondered about his father. What kind of a man was he, and why didn't La Neri live with him? Who stood in the way? She gave a little shiver and knew the answer all too well—and then as she looked at Adone her heart felt as if it turned right over inside her and for a fleeting, incredible moment she seemed to see the shades and angles of another's features in the face of Serafina's son.

She seemed to see a likeness to Rick Lordetti, and swift mental arithmetic verified her suspicion . . . Adone could well be the son of Neri's lover!

'What is it?' Adone had caught the sharp catching of her breath, and he was staring at her face, which had a sudden shocked look that made her pupils so immense they almost swamped the tawny irises. Adone drew closer to her and in the throes of a very real

71

desperation Donna thrust him away from her and sought the handle of the car door. It opened and she slid out on shaking legs.

It was true . . . it explained everything, and it hurt like hell. Adone was Rick's son! She had seen the likeness for herself, there in the fine hard bones that combined with Serafina's facial beauty to make the young Italian so striking.

She had known . . . instinct had told her that something very basic and powerful held Rick Lordetti to a woman who was more in love with herself than she could ever be with any man. It was that years ago she had borne him a son who hadn't the remotest idea that he was in any way related to Rick.

As Adone approached her from the other side of the Maserati she saw even in the way he walked, erect yet curiously graceful, his likeness to the man he didn't even like. He took her by the arm and Donna remembered the hard look in Rick's eyes when Adone had touched her this way in his presence.

It was awful, grating her feelings as a woman, that there should be no love between a man and his son. Rick Lordetti knew the truth and yet he seemed to have made no effort to establish a rapport with Adone. It was as if he had given all his affection to Serafina; all his strong and selfless protection to her alone. Or was that the way she wanted it? That Adone should never learn the truth but should go on believing himself the son of a sanctified marriage?

It seemed more than likely, Donna realised, in view of the old Hollywood system, that idolised stars should always seem glamorous and romantic, with never a hint of scandal in their lives.

Donna entered the restaurant with Adone, a tilt to her chin and a resolute smile in her eyes, and she was aware of people turning to watch them as they were shown to a table overlooking the harbour and that distant watch-tower. Adone smiled at her as they took their seats—her answering smile wasn't quite steady, for now she would always see Rick in Adone, as he had been all those years ago, carrying a terrible vengeance in his heart which one dark night he had finally satisfied.

While Adone discussed the wine list with the waiter she glanced away from the cosy interior of the restaurant out towards that lonely watch-tower standing sentinel among the rocks. It looked cold out there and bleak, and her fingers clenched on the table, forcing themselves not to jerk away when Adone covered her hand with his.

'These other people think we are lovers,' he murmured. 'Did you see the way they looked at us—we must look good together, *cara.*'

'Please, can't we talk about something else?' she spoke with a touch of exasperation. 'Let's just enjoy ourselves.'

'Then let us discuss the menu,' he smiled. 'Would you like smoked ham to start with, or perhaps sole with avocado sauce—now that sounds tempting?'

'You choose for me, Adone.'

'You are putting yourself in my hands, eh?'

'Yes—if you like.'

'I do like.' His eyes were upon her face instead of the menu. 'I like just about everything, even the reserve behind which you protect your heart. I find it exciting, challenging that you have not yet let a man into your heart.'

Donna gave him a composed look in reply, but inside herself she had never felt so disturbed and nervy. 'Do they really call this the Saracen coast?' she asked, determined to change the subject.

He nodded. 'You see the watch-tower out there, which these days is used to guide the fishing boats past those rocks. Many years ago it was used as a lookout for the Saracen pirates who came raiding this coastline, and directly the signal was received that a pirate craft had been sighted the people would speedily hide away their valuables and their daughters.' Adone broke into a smile. 'It has its amusing side, for sometimes those strictly reared girls were quite happy to be carried off, away from the suitors their parents had chosen for them. It was too often the case that only the older men were able to afford

74

a bride, and girls prefer young virile sweethearts, eh?'

'It isn't always the case that an older man lacks virility,' she rejoined. 'My father was a very attractive man to women when he was past fifty.'

'The romantic father who has taught you to search for true grit and honour.' Adone took a bread stick and bit into it with his firm white teeth. 'Are you not setting for yourself an impossibly high standard, *cara?* There are other—virtues.'

'Such as?' She gave him a challenging look.

'A warm and passionate nature, and a certain instinct for what women like. Sometimes the man of integrity is a cold stick of a puritan who has no real understanding of women. Often he prefers the devout nun-like sort who will only make demands on his soul. You can't want a man like that?' Adone's eyes were deeply green and sensual. 'Not a girl like you!'

'You barely know me. And I happen to think that those who make sacrifices make life worth living for other people.'

'How very noble of them.' He gave a mocking laugh. 'What if the main ingredient is missing when you do find this paragon of virtue? What if you aren't attracted to him physically? It happens to be important, you know. Could you give yourself to a man without wanting him in every sort of way?'

'No——' She had said it before she could stop herself, and he laughed at her, knowing he had trapped her into revealing that she could never be satisfied with a tepid relationship but would need to be on fire for a man. As the hot colour came into her cheeks, Adone's laughter melted to a soft vibration in his throat.

'I know you, *la favorita*. Before you could think of marriage you would want to be in love—very much in love. *Che bello,* that is something for a man to anticipate, but right now we shall enjoy our sole in avocado sauce, eh?'

Oh yes, she thought, her cheeks cooling over the sole, there was a devil-charm to Adone that came from Rick Lordetti . . . she had never felt so convinced of it!

She thought of Rick that night in Rome, and the way they had danced, his arms holding her close to him, his eyes meeting hers through the slits of a black mask that added devilment to his lean Sicilian face.

Had they never met again she would have gone on remembering him as a mysterious and gallant stranger, who had kissed her hand and left a white rose to remind her that their meeting could have led to more than dancing.

They had both been aware of the chemistry . . . they both knew that it still simmered in their veins each time his eyes met hers; swift, stolen glances that Serafina had not yet intercepted. Donna knew well enough that the danger was there, of falling in love with a man who was far removed from the romantic idealist of her dreams.

A man whose roots and loyalties were inextricably tied up in another woman . . . a beautiful woman he would never give up for a girl who came to work at the Villa Imperatore for a few fleeting weeks.

Chapter Four

There was always plenty of dictation on the tape-recorder for Donna to transcribe on paper. La Neri was obviously a woman who didn't sleep very well at night, for that was when she seemed at her most reminiscent, and because she had a flair for dramatic detail Donna found herself involved in her work without any effort.

Listening to Serafina on tape she could understand why a man might become enslaved by her. She had a warm, caressing voice with a charming tinge of accent, and according to her revelations a number of famous men had tried to win her favours, and not all of them in the world of films. There had been shipping tycoons, influential politicians, and wealthy bankers.

She spoke of the jewels they had showered on her, and the furs she had rejected because she despised the slaughter of beautiful animals. Few women, she said, could match the leopard for grace, the tiger for beauty, or the baby seal for endearing charm. Some men in her opinion came close to matching the lithe power of the leopard, but the ones she had in mind had not been met in Hollywood but in her native Italy. According to La Neri the men of her own country had more charm, courtesy and sensuality than most of the screen idols, and it was significant, she stated, that one of the most successful charmers had been an Italian.

Donna smiled to herself, and then looked thoughtful. Serafina was being amazingly frank with her opinions, but there were curious blanks in the early sections of the book—details of her girlhood left unstated, so the impression was of something tantalisingly withheld.

Not once did she refer in any way to Rick Lordetti, and Donna thought she knew why. When the book was completed Adone would read his mother's memoirs, and she was determined to conceal the true facts of his birth. No one but Rick was aware of that secret, and Donna had guessed because of the likeness to Rick which she had glimpsed in Adone's features. In some ways it was an explosive secret. The gossips would have a field day if it came out that La Neri was intimately acquainted with her bodyguard.

Donna's dexterous fingers paused on the typewriter keys and inevitably she thought of herself in Rick's arms, there beneath the coloured prisms that spun over the masked dancers while the orchestra played *Dream Lover*. The remembered thrill of dancing with him could not be denied, and she heard again that gravelly voice as they walked on the terrace of the ballroom. He had played a kind of game with her; made her feel the romantic fatalism of two people who met by chance but who would never meet again.

Her fingers clenched the edge of the desk and she wanted to feel angry with him for putting on such an act when he had known all the time who she was and that she was on her way to work for his . . . mistress.

He had stormed her defences that night and driven out the caution with which she usually treated strangers who tried to get acquainted with her. He had charmed her in a way she had never known before, and right now she was finding it hard to forgive him. Suddenly she couldn't bear to listen to Serafina's voice, and after switching off the recorder she walked restlessly to the long glass doors and out upon the patio of the dark knight. She was halfway across the small courtyard before she became aware of someone leaning against the trunk of a mulberry tree, half hidden among the leafy branches where the pearly silk eggs glimmered, tendrils of cigarette smoke drifting out from the foliage.

Her steps faltered, but she was too close to

the nonchalant smoker for retreat to look casual, and fighting with her sense of panic she proceeded towards the iron seat near the figure of the knight and sat down as if taking a short rest from her labours.

'I missed you at dinner last night,' Rick drawled.

'I worked, *signore,* and had dinner on a tray. We had problems with the fifth chapter and it had to be re-typed.'

'I hope you aren't being overworked? The *signora* can be forgetful of other people's feelings.'

'I didn't mind. The book is really going rather well.'

'You look rather pale from where I'm standing.'

Donna glanced at him before she could stop herself and she saw the glint of gold against his black hair, and noticed that he was wearing a dark silk shirt, corded breeches and high-laced riding boots. His gaze held hers and neither of them spoke for a few tense moments.

'Don't!' Donna wanted to beg of him. 'Leave me alone if we can't be friends openly!'

'What you need is a glass of *vino rosa,*' he said. 'We say in this part of the country that our rose wine would warm the heart of a statue. Tell me, does the stone knight intrigue you? Does he perhaps make you think of the story of the marble figure that came to life in the moonlight and made its way to a nearby cottage where a young woman was sitting at the window?'

'He left behind a marble finger,' Donna said, for she had read the horrific story.

'Gothic romance has a strange hold on the imagination, has it not?'

'All romance should be confined to the imagination,' she replied, a trifle primly.

'It is safer there, eh? A young woman can weave fantasies around a stone knight and not have to mind about his faults or his demands. What if the black knight stirred one night and climbed to your balcony. Would you scream and rouse the household?'

Donna sat there staring across at Rick and though she saw that his eyes were having wicked fun with her, she felt certain there had been a deep, meaning note in his voice. She rose to her feet and hurried past him into the office . . . instantly she caught the tramp of his riding boots as he followed her and sauntered in through the open glass doors. Taut with nerves, she stood at bay against the desk, and if she had cried out: 'Don't you dare touch me!' it couldn't have been more apparent what she was thinking.

He gave his gravelly laugh and glanced lazily about the room, looking big and powerful in his dark shirt and corded breeches, those hefty boots laced against his strong legs.

He had a look of lean, leashed danger about him; a man who had not been youthful for years but who would retain his present look for a long time to come.

'I want to touch you quite a lot,' he drawled, reading her mind with consummate ease. 'I've thought of little else since that night in Rome.'

'Please go away!'

'There's no need to look quite so wide-eyed with trepidation,' he mocked. 'I haven't entered your bedroom, sweetheart. In here I can always pretend to be giving my opinion on the opus. Am I mentioned in it?'

Donna shook her head, and wished it was possible for her to be in Rick Lordetti's presence without feeling so disturbed by the way he looked and the things he said . . . in everything he said to her there seemed a double meaning, as if she wasn't meant to take seriously anything he might imply.

He turned from a painting on the wall and gave her a lazily intent look, his eyelids drooping as if heavy with those dark lashes. 'If you were writing about me, what sort of a man would you say I was?'

Donna considered only briefly before replying. 'The kind who would walk to the gallows smoking a cigarette.'

'They wouldn't let me.' His eyes narrowed as he looked at her. 'They tie a man's hands behind him and place a cowl over his head.'

She gave a noticeable shiver, and at once he picked up the mouthpiece of the telephone on the desk and asked to be put through to the kitchen. Instead of coffee, he said, the Signorina Lovelace was to be brought a glass of *vino rosa* with her mid-morning snack. '*Si,* the Mount Etna *rosa* from the Sicilian grapes. *Grazie.*'

'You didn't have to do that,' Donna protested, colour coming into her cheeks.

'Perhaps not,' he shrugged, 'but I felt like it. I would join you in a glass of the wine, but Serafina will be expecting me to join her in a short while.'

Words that seemed to have barbed tips so that Donna almost flinched away from him. Of course, it was only to be expected that Serafina came first with him. It might amuse him to flirt a little with the hired help, but he had no intention of causing La Neri any real distress.

'You are liking it here on the Saracen coast?' he asked casually.

'Very much, *signore.*' Donna introduced a cool politeness into her voice and saw him raise an eyebrow a fraction.

'You say that, *signorina,* but you see far more of this room than you see of the countryside. I think——' He broke off and his hard white teeth clamped his upper lip for a moment. 'I think we must arrange something —do you take siesta?'

Donna shook her head and felt the sudden leap of her heart, aware that Serafina rested religiously for a couple of hours each afternoon, no doubt for the sake of her looks and because she seemed to suffer at night from insomnia.

'What is your opinion of secret meetings?' he asked, in that casual tone of voice.

'I—I don't think they're very wise.'

'Wisdom is for the elderly and neither of us has reached that stage, even if I can give you quite a lead. Would you agree to share a little conspiracy with me?'

Donna felt dual reactions to his half-expected question. Even as she said, 'No!' she was aware of wanting quite desperately to say yes.

'You haven't given it much thought,' he mocked.

'One doesn't have to think twice about playing with fire, *signore.*'

'Quite so.' He gave her a smile that held shades of the seducing quality in Adone, whom she knew to be part of him. 'Are you so chicken-hearted, a girl who came to Italy to work among strangers?'

'That's just it—I don't want to lose my job!'

'I shall see to it that we're very discreet. Won't you trust me?'

'Girls who trust men against their better judgment get hurt.'

'So you have passed judgment on me and found me wanting, eh?' As he spoke he held her eyes insistently with his own and their dark lustre, that faint whimsical smile in their depths caught at her heart and made her want to retract . . . oh, it was unfair of him to stir up wild, dangerous longings in her.

'I—I won't get involved with you—in that way. Why can't you leave me alone? You said yourself that we should behave like strangers.'

'In front of—others,' he drawled. But his relaxed tone of voice was not reflected in the sudden tautening of his shoulders so the dark silk had stretched against their power. Into his eyes had come a demanding look that completely banished that wistful hint of humour . . . now he looked like a man set on having his own way with her.

Donna saw that look and it frightened her. 'You're arrogant,' she flung at him. 'How dare you assume that I'd want to—to meet you in secret! You belong to Serafina—you're her devoted slave!'

'I'm no woman's slave, but there are things in my life you don't know—things I don't intend to talk about.' He spoke grimly. 'Anyway, you are free to choose. You and I can meet and no one need be any the wiser, but if you haven't the nerve, or you aren't woman enough, then nothing has been lost, has it, or gained?'

'I—I've never had affairs with men——' She

heard the little choked sound in her own throat, and felt the active pain that he should take it for granted.

'I know very well you haven't!' His words cut across hers, and a curt movement of his head made the gold ring glimmer. 'Do you think I, a Sicilian, would mistake you for the sort a man might carelessly enjoy—like a slice of melon on a hot day! *Cristo dio,* have I given you that impression?'

His face had gone like stone . . . only she didn't want Rick to be of stone . . . she wanted stolen hours with him, to see him smile, to hear him talk, to pretend he was hers instead of Serafina's. She felt there was loneliness in him despite his relationship to Serafina, a woman possessive of the men who belonged to her, demanding of their attention, and yet somehow devoid of a passionate warmth of heart.

'Isn't it an affair you're asking for, Rick?'

'No—damn it!' He raked a hand through his hair so a black strand fell across his fore-head. 'Do you remember that night in Rome? That is all I wanted—I swear it!'

'Oh, Rick——' The impulse to give in to him was like a wave sweeping over Donna and she wanted to throw herself into his arms . . . from that night in Rome a spark had been ignited and it had been smouldering ever since, but to be alone with him would only fan the flame and if they were ever caught together by

Serafina there would be a terrible scene. He belonged to her and nothing was going to alter the fact.

'Don't look like that!' He took a step towards her and as if control of his hands was suddenly beyond him, he caught hold of her, crushed her waist, and the next moment had her locked against him. She went strangely boneless and it was at once the most frightening and yet exciting sensation she had ever felt. And it was inevitable what happened . . . their lips met wildly until she pulled her head away.

'Rick—please!'

'Be quiet!' He caught her by the hair and pulled her face to his once more.

'You aren't being fair——'

'In the name of heaven, do I have to shut you up!' His mouth closed demandingly on hers and after some initial struggle she suddenly gave in to what his kiss was doing to her . . . Rick, oh, this was Rick, and they clung in hungry abandonment.

'We knew it had to happen sooner or later,' he muttered against her throat. 'I was fooling you and myself if I ever thought we could be alone together and not have this happen. You're so sweet and I can't be noble where you're concerned. You'll have to try and forgive me, Donna, but I can't not kiss you.'

She didn't try to stop him, her hair tangling in his fingers as he kissed her neck, the most defenceless part of a woman, making her go weak and shivery as he buried his lips into the softness behind her ear. Suddenly he groaned into the soft hollow and drew himself away from her. 'I don't just lust after you, you believe that, don't you? You must believe it, Donna.'

'I do believe it, Rick.'

He drew a ragged sigh and dragged a hand down his face. 'Will you forgive me?'

'There isn't anything to forgive,' she assured him. 'I—I joined in the kissing, didn't I?'

He smiled and looked her up and down. 'You would hardly be a match for someone my size. But I am glad you didn't entirely resist me—that I wasn't being entirely the lusting brute.'

'Oh, Rick, don't use those terrible words!'

'They are fearful, eh?' His eyes brooded upon her, then suddenly he reached out and stroked the soft hair away from her eyes. 'You had better tidy your hair, *cara*. You look—kissed.'

At once she flushed and hastened around the desk to take her comb and vanity-case out of a drawer. She heard Rick laugh in that gravelly way of his. 'I don't want to make trouble for you, *cara compaziente*.'

Donna's hand shook a little as she combed her hair and rearranged it, and they both knew what had come into the room to join them, the inevitable feeling of guilt because he wasn't free, could never be free to kiss another woman in Serafina's house.

Donna had just put away her comb and mirror when the door opened and there, as if in a frame, stood the woman whose hold on Rick was like a chain he could never break. She wore a velvet morning-gown in silvery green, long-skirted, with draped sleeves and a heart-shaped bodice. Her hair was unbound about her shoulders and in the sunlight that came through the patio doors Donna saw the unexpected threads of silver in La Neri's glistening hair.

When her green eyes settled on Rick, he was lounging against the corner of the desk with some sheets of typescript in his hand, while with the other hand he was applying the flame of his lighter to a cigarette.

'So here you are!' Serafina gave him a sharp look, which he returned lazily, the dark lashes making his eyes look darker. 'I've been waiting for you for the past ten minutes— what are you doing?'

'Being inquisitive,' he drawled, a thread of smoke drifting from his nostrils. 'You don't imagine you could write a book, *carissima,* and not arouse my curiosity?'

'About what?' she demanded.

'Many things.'

She gave a petulant shrug and turned her gaze on Donna, her eyes as hard and gleaming as green glass as they swept the figure of her secretary in pale linen with discreet touches of turquoise. Donna looked outwardly composed, but her heart was pounding. Her nerves quivered as she imagined the proportions of the scene had La Neri swept in while Rick was kissing her.

'I thought you wore spectacles to work in,' she snapped at Donna. 'Did you take them off in order to look attractive for the *signore?*'

'No, of course not.' The spectacles lay on a scribble-pad beside the typewriter, placed there when Donna had gone out on to the patio and encountered Rick. She wished to heaven she had stayed in here, then he wouldn't have followed her from the patio and they wouldn't have finished up in each other's arms.

Donna felt as guilty as if they had been caught in that embrace, but Rick looked as nonchalant as he had beneath the mulberry tree, as if it wasn't the first time he had kissed a girl behind Serafina's back.

'Don't be sharp with Miss Lovelace because I've taken the liberty of reading some of your manuscript.' He drew on his cigarette and looked intently at Serafina, and Donna saw something in his eyes that startled her . . . a look of command that was far removed from the gaze of a compliant lover or a paid bodyguard. It was there for a brief moment, but it made Donna realise that he wasn't under La Neri's thumb at all but was probably more her master than she was his mistress.

Donna's fingers clenched the spectacles which she had picked up, and it now seemed ridiculous that she had ever imagined that a man like Rick sacrificed his real dreams and desires and devoted himself to Serafina out of a sense of loyalty. The truth struck Donna that he was the real power at the villa; that he controlled La Neri and her fortune and was far from being her slave. She should have realised it right away . . . hadn't he said himself that he was no woman's slave?

'Your book will have a wide appeal, *carissima.*' He gave that quirk of a smile and Donna tried to ignore the way Serafina responded, throwing out a hand to him which he pressed a moment to his lips. A stab of jealousy struck Donna under the heart and she wished she could hate him and not be so strirred up by his every action, his every look, which were all part of the expertise of a man who deceived his mistress even as he kept her enslaved by him.

Oh yes, Donna could see it now, and her hands shook as she placed carbons between sheets of manuscript paper. Serafina was the slave, not Rick Lordetti!

'You truly believe it will be a best-seller?' The sensual tones of La Neri's voice were overlaid by a tremor. 'I am only concerned with telling people about my career, Rick.

That is the best way, eh? None of the shadows but only the spotlights, as on a film set.'

'By far the best way,' he agreed. 'Your memoirs, *carissima,* should be as beautiful as you are.'

'*Caro mio,* you always make me feel as lovely and desirable as I was in the old days—ah, those days, Rick, that fill my heart with so much emotion!' The slim elegant hands wrapped themselves about his shoulders, holding him as if no one else existed for her, and Donna had to watch and suffer the painful knowledge that no one could possess him as this beautiful woman did. Her hands clung to him with a kind of helpless need, as if he were the strong staff she leaned on and couldn't live without.

They were standing like that when there was a polite knock on the door and it opened to admit the young footman with Donna's mid-morning tray. The sunlight caught the gleam of rosy wine in the stemmed glass and even as Donna noticed it, Serafina was giving the wine glass a sharp glance.

'What is this?' she demanded of Enrico. 'Who has ordered wine to be brought to the workroom?'

'It was I who ordered it,' Rick explained. 'Miss Lovelace has been looking rather pale— you have to admit, *cara,* that she has been working hard on your book and had a meal on a tray last night.'

Serafina shot a glance at Donna that was suddenly so hostile that it made her eyes look cat-cruel. 'The girl came here to work,' she said cuttingly, 'not to be mollycoddled! Have you been complaining to the *signor* that I am overworking you, Miss Lovelace?'

'Indeed not!' Donna looked indignant. 'I didn't ask for the wine, and I daresay it's my lack of a suntan that makes me look pale.'

'Are you now suggesting, Miss Lovelace, that you are kept for such long hours at the typewriter that I am depriving you of sunning yourself in your bikini, your slim English body on display for the men of my household?'

Donna flushed, half in anger. 'I never wear a bikini——'

'Ah, you mean you like to lie in the sun in your bare skin?'

'No, I don't! I consider the bikini an ugly garment, and I quite agree that I came here to work. It has never crossed my mind, *signora,* to behave at the villa as if I were a guest. I enjoy my work, and I'm certainly not complaining about anything.'

'I am gratified to hear you say that,' Serafina snapped, 'for I intend to keep you as busy as it suits me. I am paying you an excellent salary, and in future you will not expect to drink wine while you are working.'

Donna's temper flared right up and she felt an impulse to take hold of the wineglass and toss the contents out on the patio pavement. She hadn't wanted the wretched drink in the first place, and something of what she felt must have leapt into her eyes for Rick took hold of Serafina and propelled her towards the door. 'What a lot of fuss over such a small matter,' he chided her. 'Your cellar is stocked with enough wine to intoxicate the crew of a battleship and you get petulant because just a little of it is served to a young woman who works hard for you. It isn't like you to be so inhospitable.'

Serafina ran searching eyes over his face, and a moment before she departed the office she turned to look again at Donna, and the green eyes were still hostile and sharp with suspicion. Donna's nerves gave a jolt and she felt as if it were showing that she had been ardently kissed by the man whom La Neri considered her sole property.

The door closed and Donna was thankfully alone, the sunlight turning the *vino rosa* to a glowing ruby colour. Donna felt as if it would have choked her, and yet she knew in her heart that Rick had meant to be kind. Oh God—she sank her face into her hands and felt so confused, so torn between liking him and believing him to be an experienced rake who played with the feelings of silly young innocents like herself. She hadn't wanted to feel this way about any man, least of all a man much older than herself whom she could never hope to have.

She felt haunted by the things Adone had told her about Rick . . . about his mother and the vengeance he had taken upon her killer. Such terrible events would have helped to make him the way he was, scarring his mind and hardening his heart.

Donna wondered if Serafina had ever possessed the tenderness to ease the pain of his memories. She had her great beauty, the seductiveness of her body, the charisma of her stardom . . . yet in appealing to Donna for a little of what they had found together that night in Rome Rick revealed a certain emptiness in his life; a need for some quality unpossessed by La Neri.

Or was she being hopelessly naïve and romantic about this man . . . killer, gambler, lover of another woman? Donna reached out and ran a finger around the rim of the wine glass . . . a wine to warm the heart of a statue, he had said, but hers was vibrantly alive in her warm body, responsive to the very thought of him even as her mind warned her that to care for Rick Lordetti was to play a dangerous game.

She shivered convulsively and carried the glass of wine to her lips. It was faintly sweet and potently warming as it wended its way through her veins. There would have been a bittersweet pleasure to sharing a few stolen hours with Rick, but she must keep her distance from him while she remained at the Villa Imperatore; she must not run the risk of letting him kiss her again.

That look in La Neri's eyes had been sharp as a blade, as if she might be capable of using a stiletto on anyone who dared to try and take Rick away from her. The bond between them had been forged long ago . . . he belonged to her, the woman who was Adone's mother.

Chapter Five

It was a glorious morning, with golden sunlight spilling across the bed as Donna awoke and stretched her limbs in her flimsy nylon nightdress. She gazed upwards at the sunlight as it moved across the painted ceiling of her bedroom, gilding the angelic faces peering around fluffy white clouds, curvaceous limbs and shoulders just showing. After five weeks she had grown very fond of this room, with its hand-woven curtains and glossy rattan furniture. Through an adjoining archway there was a small *sala,* with a bookcase, a desk and a small curving couch. And there was also a small balcony that jutted above the stables, although Donna didn't mind the smell of horses but knew it was the reason she had this otherwise attractive pair of rooms.

Quite often there were guests at the villa and Donna could see them trotting the glossy-coated horses along the flagstone path that led into the hills. What fascinated her was to see

Serafina riding sidesaddle, clad in a moss-green riding habit and a small bowler-like hat that made her look like some beautiful Edwardian print which had come to life. It was a costume she had worn in one of her favourite films and because she was La Neri she lived and loved and rode her black mare just as it suited her.

When Serafina went riding, Rick went with her, clad in a corduroy jacket and well-worn corded breeches, with the high-laced boots a *contadino* might wear. Did he ever think of his parents' olive farm on the isle of Sicily? Donna wondered. Did he ever have dreams that La Neri would never want to share with him?

They made a striking pair, and Donna had thought she was unobserved up on her balcony, half concealed by drapings of foliage, until late one afternoon when hoofbeats came along the path to the stables and then abruptly paused right under the jut of her balcony.

'Donna!'

It wasn't the voice of a youthful Romeo, for it grated in a very masculine throat, and it also demanded that she reveal herself from where she sat in a rattan chair, half hidden by the wine-coloured bougainvilleas that grew so abundantly over the framework of her balcony.

Donna remained where she was and told

herself that he would ride on in a moment, and then she tensed as the hoofs clattered a little closer. 'I know you're up there,' he said. 'And I feel confident the branches of this magnolia will take my weight—shall I climb up?'

'No!' She jumped to her feet and moved to the edge of the balcony, and there below in the reddening glow of the sunset he sat astride his big handsome bay that swished its tail in a certain impatience to get to its oats.

Rick gazed up at her with a slightly derisive smile. 'I feel sure Juliet didn't react in that timid way when Romeo wanted to climb to her balcony.'

'Perhaps Juliet didn't have visions of a slim boy breaking his neck before he reached the balcony,' Donna retorted.

'Ah, concerned for my safety, *carina?*'

'Don't call me that!' Her hands clenched the balcony rail. 'Save your endearments for the Signora Neri, who wouldn't be very pleased if she caught you talking to me in this way.'

'As a matter of fact I wished to apologise for the way she spoke to you that morning in the office. I hope you understood——'

'Only too well, *signore*. She suspected that you were paying me some attention and she didn't like it. It was perfectly natural—she obviously cares for you and depends on you, and I certainly don't want to be the cause of any friction between you. I would prefer to be left alone—by you.'

'By me, but not by Adone, eh? You have been getting quite friendly with him, haven't you? The other evening songs at the piano, and you play quite well, don't you? What is it this evening? Have you made your plans?'

'He's taking me to a dance on the yacht of a friend.' Donna tried to speak casually, but she couldn't quite keep the tremor out of her voice—even to think of dancing was to recall every detail of being held in Rick's arms while the music played. She had tried . . . tried desperately to think of Adone as being Rick all over again, but it hadn't really worked, and she knew as she gazed down at Rick in the deepening dusk that she would have loved to dance with him on the deck of a yacht as it rocked at anchor and the sound of the sea mingled with the music. She wanted to be close to the hard warmth of him; every inch of her skin clamoured for contact with him, and having to deny herself that gratification was more painful than anything she had ever experienced. A physical ache could be dealt with, but it wasn't so easy when it came to soothing heartache.

'I hope you will be careful in his company, Donna.' Rick's face had gone as hard as iron and the big bay shifted sideways as if fingers had tightened on his bridle. 'Adone is a very experienced young man and he knows how to turn on the charm. I wouldn't want to see you come to any harm when you go dancing on this yacht. He has friends who don't altogether meet with my approval.'

'How stuffy you sound!' Donna forced herself to laugh. 'I would have said that you are far more dangerous than your—than Adone could ever be.'

Rick's eyes narrowed and she saw them glittering even as the darkness was creeping over his face and figure. Her heart jerked and she prayed that he hadn't noticed the slip of the tongue she had almost made.

'I have known Adone all his life,' Rick said curtly. 'You have been acquainted with him only a few weeks. He has a wild strain in his blood and he likes his own way. I have seen the way he has looked at you. I have seen desire in his eyes!'

Donna had noticed before that when Rick gave in to a certain emotional feeling his English became far more Latin . . . Donna was ready to believe there was a dangerous strain in Adone, and she knew from whom he had inherited his self-will, and his strong passions. They came from Rick, as did his bone structure.

'You don't have to concern yourself about me, *signore*,' Donna said, making herself sound cool and casual . . . making believe it didn't thrill her deep down that Rick was jealous of her friendship with Adone. 'I can take care of myself, and I believe Adone has learned to respect my feelings.'

'And what are those, Donna?' Rick spoke demandingly. 'Don't lead that young man on if you don't intend to fulfill his—expectations.'

'What do you mean by that?' she gasped.

'I should think my meaning is clear enough. You aren't a child, and neither is Adone, and you might be wise to stay away from this party——'

'Don't dictate to me!' Donna was furious with him for assuming he had the right to tell her what to do. 'You neither employ me nor own me, and in my spare time I shall go exactly where I please. Save you dictatorial attitude for your—for Serafina.'

'I am well aware that I have no rights with regard to you,' he said. 'But I don't want to see you get—hurt.'

'I rather fancy, Signor Lordetti, that I stood more chance of that if I had run the risk of seeing you behind Serafina's back. I daresay it's a game you have often played and I suppose you're annoyed because I refused to join in. I can go out openly with Adone. I thought his mother might object, but as she doesn't——'

'Serafina has never refused Adone anything he has fancied,' Rick rejoined, his voice on the edge of harshness. 'Her attitude is that if he fancies to play around with the English Miss, then by all means let him, and for what it's worth, Donna, there have been a number of girls in Adone's life—they are toys to him!'

'And what are they to you?' she demanded. 'Do you envy Adone his freedom to enjoy himself openly?'

'Freedom is quite a word, isn't it?' A note of heaviness had come into Rick's voice, as if a kind of weight lay on his spirit. 'You have it, Donna, but in the name of *Cristo* don't trade it in for regret. That can come so easily to a young girl, and for the rest of her life she has to live with it.'

'I suppose, Rick, I wouldn't be laying in regret for myself had I agreed to clandestine meetings with you?' As she spoke Donna gripped the iron rail in front of her, needing the outer pain to try and offset the inner one. 'What are you worried about? That I shall get into trouble with Adone the way Serafina got into trouble with—his father?'

'God in heaven, no!' It was a husky exclamation down there in the gathering darkness which Donna barely caught. The pain struck at her nerves rather than her ears and she felt the torment that wrenched the words from him. There was an abrupt silence between them, filled in by the *cigales* in the trees and by the jingle of the bay's bridle as he moved his head, scenting the nearby stables and wanting to get home to his supper.

'How did you guess?' Rick asked suddenly. 'No one could have told you—you're making a wild guess!'

'Adone is like you—didn't you know?' Donna's lips were so dry that it hurt her to speak. 'Haven't you ever seen yourself in him?'

Again there was a void of shocked silence, with only the sound of the *cigales* pulsating in the air. 'Perhaps I have tried to avoid seeing myself in that young profligate.' Rick spoke harshly. 'If you have any sense you will keep out of his clutches, but as we have both agreed I have no dominion over your life and you are free to stretch your wings. Take care of them, won't you? There's no way for a girl to fly to the stars once her young and shining wings are broken.'

The hooves of his mount clattered on the path as he turned the bay in the direction of the stables. They cantered away, and now the darkness was complete . . . it even felt as if it had crept into Donna's heart.

She withdrew from the balcony into her small private *sala,* and there with a shiver she lit the lamps. It seemed awful to her that Rick should feel no affection for Adone, and see in him only the faults of his own youth. It was as if he had never wanted to associate himself with the birth or the upbringing of Serafina's son, whom she had left in the hands of a compliant, much older husband. Where was that husband now? Did he exist at all, or had he been invented to provide a background of respectability for Serafina?

Donna sat down on the rattan couch and cradled a cushion against her. Suddenly she felt quite certain that Serafina had never been married to anyone. Someone had been well paid to take care of Adone until she was ready to have him share her home . . . the only man in La Neri's life was Rick Lordetti.

Always . . . from the beginning . . . and it suited them to pretend to the world that he was only her bodyguard.

Yes, that was the way Serafina would want to live, as if her life was a dramatic screenplay. No doubt both she and Rick liked the danger inherent in their way of living, he the stern, tough *castellan* who carried a gun, holstered beneath his well-cut jacket. It was more exciting for a woman who was an actress to her fingertips, and much more of a deterrent to kidnappers, the publicity built up around La Neri and her bodyguard, a man with the chilling reputation of having killed a member of the dreaded Mafia.

Donna drew a shaky sigh . . . perhaps she should do as Rick suggested and cancel her date with Adone. She didn't really want to go to this yacht party, for she was aware that his kind of friends were not her kind. Most of them had money and were merely intent on enjoying life, and those who didn't have money of their own were adept at gambling or borrowing it so they could have fun.

She went into her bedroom and after lighting the lamps in there, drew her fingers down the flowing skirt of the dress she had already hung on the door of the wardrobe. She could always excuse herself with a headache, and yet if she did so she would be giving in to Rick. Giving in to a man who had no right to try and run her life. If Adone was spoiled and addicted to pleasure, then Rick was half to blame. He had never tried to stop Serafina from always giving in to Adone, of paying his debts and shrugging her shoulders at his misdeeds. She adored him and saw her own outstanding beauty reflected in his handsome face.

Restless, torn with doubts, Donna wandered about her room, giving a nervous start when the pretty Limoges clock began to chime. Adone had asked her to be ready by seven-thirty, and she had only half an hour in which to shower and dress . . . if she went with him and didn't find some excuse to let him down.

She drew her bottom lip between her teeth and felt hesitant . . . if she broke this date, then she knew what Adone would do at the party. He would drink too much, probably get into a card game and lose too much, and spend the remainder of the night with a woman who was bored with her husband. Donna had no illusions about Adone, but she was aware that he had led a more temperate life since she had started going out with him.

She quite liked him, even if she couldn't pretend that he was Rick. Darn Rick! Why did he have to intrude into everything . . . her thoughts and feelings, and her heart itself!

More from defiance than actual desire, Donna gathered together her toiletries and robe and went along the gallery to the bathroom. There she quickly showered, covering her hair with a cap because she didn't have time to dry it. Talcum-powder flew and her cheeks were flushed from the warmth as she looped the sash of her robe and stepped out of the steamy bathroom . . . giving a gasp as she walked straight into someone who was going along the gallery.

As she stumbled a pair of hands caught at her, so strong that they seemed to lift her from the floor. Her eyes lifted and locked with Rick's, and time seemed to lose a beat as they stood like that, a space between their lips where their quickened breath mingled. Her eyelids seemed to grow weighted and through her lashes she saw that unruly strand of black hair meeting his left eyebrow. She hung there in his arms almost as if drowsy, a silken-dark curl to her lashes, with little wet strands against her neck. He studied her face intently, as if memorising her features and the wild flush across her cheekbones. Her heart was pounding, as if trying to get out of her body into his.

'Do you know what I'd like to do with

you?' he murmured.

She didn't need answer to him, for it was there in her eyes that she was perfectly aware of his inclinations.

His lip quirked and deep in his eyes were a pair of little flames. 'I'd like to lock you up like some Victorian guardian and see to it that you couldn't come to any harm. My advice has gone into one ear and out of the other, eh? You are going to this party, looking as fresh and innocent as some infant straight out of the soap bubbles.'

'Why are you so against this yacht party?' She just had to ask, for it wasn't the first time he had seen her going out on a date with Adone.

'The yacht is the *Dalila* and it belongs to a man I don't very much like. Several times Adone has lost money to him at card games, and I know for a fact that this man cheats. Adone is a young devil with the women, but he has his saving graces and one of them is that he hates cheats as much as I do. He hasn't yet discovered for himself that this man is a cardsharp, and there will be trouble when he does find out.'

'Then it's just as well I'm going with him to the party,' Donna said. 'He seems to behave himself when I'm around.'

'How does he behave when you're alone with him?' Rick asked, and one of his strong hands clasped her head and tilted it backwards

109

so that he could look down into her eyes, searchingly.

'Better than you do.' She had to defend herself against Rick, and to attack him seemed the best way. His eyes narrowed, and then quite suddenly he lowered his head and took her lips with his, in a couple of brief, biting kisses that made her feel as if her legs were going to give way beneath her. Then he put her away from him, and she believed it was accidental when his hand touched her body where her robe had slightly opened. She heard him catch his breath, then swinging on his heel he said curtly:

'Enjoy your evening. You probably will be safer with Adone than you would be with me!'

Donna almost ran into her bedroom, legs tremulous as she quickly closed the door behind her. She was breathing unevenly and her skin was still tingling where his hand had brushed. She had heard about this kind of physical awareness, this chemistry that was so mysterious, and so often active between two people who had no right to feel it. She pressed her hands to her burning cheeks and was suddenly aware of her body in the way a man would be aware of it, of its smoothness and slimness and youthful desirability. Rick wanted her, she had seen it in his eyes . . . and she wanted Rick to feel like that, and it was wrong, it was dangerous, and it could

110

lead to disaster.

She began to dress, but she still wasn't in full control of her nerves or her emotions. She couldn't forget the feel of Rick's mouth on hers, his reciprocation of a little cruelty because she had to be on the defensive with him, saying sharp things because she didn't dare to be tender.

Oh God, to be tender to Rick would lead to complications she didn't dare to face. She could hardly look at herself in the mirror, for what he did to her was there in her eyes . . . the glow of an excitement that enhanced her looks and even made her hair feel extra soft and silky. She wore a long honey-coloured velvet skirt and a long-sleeved silk shirt in magnolia. On her feet were slender strapped shoes, and her only jewellery was a pair of topaz eardrops. Her father had always said that she resembled her mother, and that what he had loved about the woman he had lost too early in their life together had been her style, her touch of class and natural air of reserve that concealed a very real warmth of heart.

Donna picked up the small velvet jacket that matched her skirt and draped it around her shoulders. As she made her way downstairs she hoped that Adone had already said goodnight to his mother . . . she didn't want to go into the *salone* where Rick would look at her with the knowledge in his eyes that her body had reacted to his with a desire almost equal to what he as an experienced man could feel. She felt the warmth rising in her cheeks, felt the tremor in her legs that made her grip the handrail of the stairs.

As she reached the bottom of the staircase she caught the sound of raised voices. 'Who the hell are you to put in your spoke about money?' Adone spoke in a loud, angry voice. 'You get paid your whack for being the strong-arm man everyone's afraid of, Serafina's big dark shadow who lives like a lord at her expense! But don't forget you're just an employee, Lordetti, and you'll keep that big Roman nose of yours out of my business.'

'There is no need, Adone, to get so incensed,' broke in Serafina's placating voice. 'Rick is perfectly right—you have been losing rather heavily at cards and I'm not made of money. If there is to be dancing on the yacht, why should you need more money? I gave you a cheque only a few nights ago.'

'I have a debt that has to be paid,' Adone said, his tone of voice becoming sulky. 'I don't want to get the reputation of being a bilker.'

'A bilker, *mio curo?* What is that?'

'Someone who evades payment of a gambling debt. Come on, you can afford to let me have another cheque.'

'Don't give him any more money, Serafina.' Rick spoke grimly. 'If he wants to gamble in

the kind of company that plays for dangerously high stakes, then let him earn the money
to do it with.'

'I tell you I have a debt to pay.' A note of
violent dislike had come into Adone's voice.
'And as I told you once before, Lordetti,
don't boss me around, and don't behave as if
you're the master here. You're nothing more
than a paid henchman and you imagine you
can put the fear of the devil into everyone,
only you don't happen to scare me. Oh yes, I
know all about your karate skill, and it's certainly no secret that you killed a man that
way, even if they did say he struck his head. I
daresay you could chop me down, but that
doesn't mean I shake at the knees when you
frown at me——'

'*Silenzio!*' The order came with sudden
sharpness from Serafina. 'You will not speak
to Rick in that way, and you will understand,
Adone, that even from you I will not tolerate
such insolence or mention of matters that are
in the past. You will ignore him, Rick.'

'I usually do,' Rick drawled. 'I understood,
Adone, that you were taking Miss Lovelace to
the *Dalila*. Do I also understand that there is
to be a card game down in the saloon?'

'Probably, but I need the money to pay off
my losses—don't give me that look, Lordetti.
I shall take care of Donna, if that's what is
worrying you. Is it? I've noticed you looking
at her once or twice. Pretty girl, isn't she?

Such wonderfully fair hair——'

'Shut your mouth,' Rick snapped at him. 'If I'm concerned for Miss Lovelace it's because I know the kind of company you keep. I doubt if she is accustomed to mixing with social parasites and women who fornicate like back-alley cats. She is obviously a nice girl, so be warned that she stays that way——'

It was at that point in the dispute that Donna decided to enter the *salone* and remove Adone from Rick's presence before they came to blows. Adopting a casual air and a smile, she walked into the room. 'So here you are,' she said to Adone, as if she hadn't caught a word of the wrangle. 'If we don't make a move the party will be over before we get there.'

Adone turned to her, and then with an air of possessiveness he came to her and in front of his mother, and Rick, he bent and kissed her cheek. 'You look as if you had walked in from among the flowers,' he said gallantly. He held her arm, gave his mother a little bow, and pointedly ignored Rick as he escorted Donna from the *salone*.

'I hate that damn man,' he muttered, as he opened the car door for Donna. 'I wish Serafina could be persuaded to cut loose from him, but he has such a hold on her that she seems to regard him as some kind of omnipotent force in her life.'

'I shouldn't interfere between them,' Donna

114

said carefully. 'Your mother obviously has a great need of him, and you can't say that he ever really interferes in your life.'

'He puts his grit into the oil when he feels like it, believe you me, Donna. Damn him to hell,' Adone muttered, as he started the car and they sped away from the villa with a promise of speed that made Donna grip the edge of her seat. A quick glance at Adone showed her that he was in a reckless mood, and suddenly she wished that she had taken Rick's advice and stayed at home.

'Adone——'

'What is it?' He hurled the car around a bend and the wheels made a protesting scream on the tarmac.

'I—I have a slight headache—would you mind turning back? I don't really fancy going to the party.'

'You dressed yourself up for it, and very nicely—in fact, I've never seen you look so stunning.' He flicked a look at her even as he moved his foot down on the accelerator. 'You will make those other women look like a bunch of bats who have just flown in out of the caves. They deck themselves out in diamonds and furs, but they haven't your marvellous skin and hair. Rick's jealous, do you know that? He's jealous as hell because I have you——'

'No one has me, Adone,' she broke in, feeling the quickening of her pulses because

Adone had hit so close to a probable truth. 'Because I go out with you sometimes it doesn't mean that you can take it for granted I'm your property. Please turn back. I'm really not in the mood for a party.'

'You were when I suggested it,' he rejoined. 'You said it would be fun to dance on a deck above the water. What's the matter, Donna? Did you overhear some of that argument with Rick and are you afraid I might be leading you astray? How very amusing! He's the one who could do that! He knows more about the gambling syndicates and the seamy characters who walk on the dark side of the street than I could ever know. He's a Sicilian who took an oath of vengeance, and during the years he was searching for the man he swore to kill he mixed with the dregs in every back-alley bar. A lot of it rubs off, especially on a teenager, and by the time he was my age, Lordetti was a seasoned gambler. I envy the way he can cut the cards, and you must ask him one day to throw a knife so it slices a melon at ten paces. They whisper about him in the water-front cafes. He's the man with the golden ring.'

'Who did the ring belong to?' Donna felt a compulsion to know. 'It's a wedding ring, isn't it?'

'Yes, it came from the hand of his mother. He removed it before they closed her coffin, and an old woman in the district where he

116

lived pierced a hole in his earlobe and he has worn the ring ever since. Sicilians have a strain of the dramatic in them, and they're as steeped in the vendetta as the Corsicans. That's part of his mystique for Serafina. She has played so often in romantic melodrama that she regards Rick as her big dark hero. It suits him to play along. She's still a superb-looking woman, and she's also a very rich one.'

'I'd say there's more to it than that,' Donna found herself protesting.

'What, for instance?'

'No one seeing them together could doubt that they're devoted to each other.'

'As lovers, do you mean?' Adone snarled the words. 'That's what I've never been able to tolerate; as if where my own mother is concerned I'm puritanical. Time and time again I've walked in on them, hoping to find her in his arms so I could really raise the roof, but he's foxy, as underhand as the devil, as if he has some sixth sense that always keeps him ahead of being taken by surprise. He's like a damn tiger . . . he can smell danger!'

The car roared on with angry speed towards the waterfront, until the conviction grew in Donna that they were never going to arrive there without a mishap. It was on one of the raking bends that Adone braked just in time to avoid a sprawling mass of earth and rock, probably brought down in the rainstorm of the previous night.

The Maserati skidded to a halt, and unfortunately Donna had fastened her safety-belt and was saved from jerking forward, but Adone had left his belt undone and as the car bucked to a halt he was thrown forward on to the steering wheel, and Donna heard a grunt of pain and the next instant saw blood gushing from his mouth.

She swiftly unbuckled her own belt and carefully drew his head back against the seat so she could see what he had done. 'Hurts like hell,' he mumbled, and after stemming some of the blood with his handkerchief Donna discovered that he had badly cut his bottom lip and it was bleeding copiously. She could also feel some loosened teeth.

'I've got to get you to a doctor!' she gasped, for she could see at once that his lip needed stitching. But he shook his head and held the handkerchief pressed to his mouth.

'Dentist,' he spoke through the stained linen. 'Won't lose any teeth—damned if I will! You drive. I'll direct you to his house.'

It was during the drive to the dentist that Donna felt more than ever convinced that Adone was very much a part of Rick Lordetti. He didn't whine or complain, but hung on to his severely cut lip and loosened teeth. He had fine teeth, so Donna could understand why he was concerned that they be saved if possible,

and it was with intense relief that she drew
the car to a standstill in the small courtyard
of a house along the promenade.

Donna spent the next couple of hours with
the dentist's wife, drinking coffee and waiting
anxiously for Adone to be attended to. It was
true that he had invited the accident with his
reckless driving, but she felt sorry for him and
couldn't help admiring his courage. He hadn't
panicked, and though the pain must have been
considerable he had borne it quietly. Just
before taking the dental chair he had told
Donna not to telephone his mother. 'She gets
upset,' was all he had said.

The tension was relieved when the dentist
came from the surgery to inform Donna that
the patient was resting for a few minutes and
would soon be able to see her. 'He will soon
recover,' she was assured. 'Signor Neri has excellent teeth and it would have been a pity to
lose a couple of them just for the sake of
avoiding a little more pain. His lips will
probably carry a scar, but only a slight one.
He's an extremely good-looking young man,
but it was his teeth he was mainly concerned
about. He dislikes the idea of dentures.'

Donna smiled her relief. 'It was the cut on
his lip that was worrying me. Will I be able
to drive him home?'

The dentist shook his head. 'I am going to
suggest Signor Neri remains here at my house
for the night. He is still very shaken and has

lost quite an amount of blood. I have x-rayed his jaw but there isn't any sign of a fracture, but I would like to keep him under my care and attention for the remainder of the night, and we have a spare room in which he can sleep.'

This sounded like good common sense to Donna, and when she nodded the dentist turned to his wife and requested that she make up the spare bed and put in a hot-water bottle.

'Now come along and see the *signor.*' Donna was escorted into the rest room, where Adone was stretched out on a sofa looking rather pallid and with a neat line of stitching in his lip. He held out a hand to Donna and his eyes expressed what he was at present unable to put into words. She clasped his hand and smiled down at him. 'I shall be very diplomatic when I tell your mother about the accident,' she assured him. 'Perhaps now you'll take heed of her warning and not drive so fast.'

He pressed her fingers and a smile came into his eyes as he drew her hand to his cheek and held it there. She knew instantly that he was begging a little sympathy even though he knew he'd risked both their lives. Donna leaned down and gently kissed his face. 'Are you still in pain?' she murmured. 'I understand from the dentist that fixing those teeth was no picnic, and on top of that you had to

120

be stitched. Are you quite comfortable? Are you truly feeling better, or is it still bad?'

He shook his head and Donna guessed that his mouth was numb at the moment but would be sore when the effects of the injection had worn off. 'Get some sleep,' she urged him. 'I expect your mother will come and fetch you home in the morning.'

He frowned slightly, and Donna added quickly: 'I know you'd like me to come for you, but she'll want to fuss over you a little. It's her right, Adone.'

He gripped her hand as if he'd like to keep her with him, but Donna drew away from him until he had to release her. 'I must go,' she said. 'See you tomorrow. *Arrivederci!*'

Back in the sitting-room Donna caught sight of the telephone and wondered if she ought to put a call through to the villa. She could speak to Rick. Ask him to explain to Serafina that Adone had suffered a slight accident . . . no, when one spoke the word 'accident' over the telephone it always sounded far more ominous than it should, and it wouldn't do Adone a lot of good if Serafina insisted upon coming down to the dental surgery tonight. He needed to get some uninterrupted rest, and would be a lot better in the morning . . . more able to cope with her anxiety.

'Thank you for all you have done.' Donna shook hands with dentist and his wife, and they watched her from the doorway of their house as she drove away in the Maserati. She made for the mountain road, and though her nerves still felt a trifle shaky, she felt confident she could handle the car on those undulating gradients. It was that rock fall she had to be careful to avoid, and she forced all her concentration upon her driving, keeping the headlights at full force so she would see that mound of dirt and rock before she drove into it.

Donna estimated that she was about halfway home when the engine suddenly stalled and she found herself pressing the starter button to no avail at all. Some kind of engine damage must have occurred when Adone had swerved the car and brought it to that jarring halt which had thrown him on to the wheel.

'Dammit!' Donna sat there, with the headlights splayed out across the road. She wasn't on a bend, thank goodness, or the Maserati would have been a hazard to any vehicle driving down. But she was stranded in the car and had to admit to herself that she didn't fancy walking the rest of the way to the villa. She felt tempted to remain inside the car where she could lock the doors and snuggle down beneath the lap-robe which lay on the back seat. It would be assumed at the villa that she and Adone were staying overnight on the yacht, and as soon as it was daylight she could walk home without feeling nervous of the dark twisting road and what might be lurking among the trees that crowded the slopes.

The longer Donna stayed inside the car the more reluctant she became to step outside and start walking. Just to test the density of the night she switched off the headlights, and as the darkness fell around her the nerves crawled along her spine.

It was no use! She was still on edge from what had happened to Adone and couldn't face that dark journey on foot. She would settle down on the back seat of the car and feel quite secure with the doors locked.

Donna sank her head against the back of her seat and wished she had taken notice of Rick . . . the entire evening had been a disaster, and instead of being safe in her comfortable bedroom at the villa she was stranded here in the dark. Suddenly, without warning, there swept over her the wish that Rick was here to make the night feel less lonely. Rick, who challenged her as no one else had ever done; who sometimes teased her as if she were a small girl, and then treated her as if she were a woman he very much desired.

Far down on the water Donna could see the lights of the fishing boats, and way above her in the sky shone the stars which a girl might reach on young and shining wings . . . so Rick had said. A girl in love, he had meant. A girl who didn't give her love away as if it had no value. A girl who kept her heart and her body for the one and only man.

That man could never be Rick . . . she had to accept what Adone had said of him, that he had walked too long on the dark side of the street to be able to look at the sunlight with untroubled eyes. For now and always he had linked his life with that of a woman who was like him and understood him. It would be folly . . . it would be asking for a broken heart to ever dream that she could fit into his life. When her work was finished at the Villa Imperatore they would say goodbye.

'Rick . . .' she sighed, and fell asleep in a car she had forgotten to lock.

Chapter Six

It was the touch of a hand that awoke Donna and she sat up with a cry, dazed and cold with an ache in her neck from the angle at which she had fallen asleep.

The car door was open and the figure of a man was leaning in towards her . . . instinctively she flung out a hand to push him away, and then he spoke and caught her by the shoulders. 'It's all right, Donna. You are quite safe with me.'

'Rick!' She stopped struggling and realised that it was faintly light enough for her to see his face. Dark, strong, reassuring. 'Oh, Rick, you gave me such a scare!'

'I gather you had trouble with the car. Why didn't you lock the doors, eh? It was a little risky falling asleep with them unlocked.'

'I—I forgot.' She looked about her and saw that the intense darkness of the night had given way to the pallor of early morning. 'What time is it, and what are you doing here?'

He shot the cuff of his trench coat and took a look at his watch. 'It's just on five o'clock, and I would like to know what you are doing here in a stalled car. Do I take it Adone is still on the yacht and that you ran out on him?'

'No.' Donna sat there rubbing the back of her neck and looking at Rick with bemused eyes. 'Tell me why you're here.'

'Serafina couldn't sleep and wanted coffee. I made her some and then, curious to see if Adone had yet brought you home, I took the liberty of glancing into your room. When I saw your empty bed I jumped to the conclusion that you were on the yacht with him, and I was coming down to fetch you home. And now you will explain what you are doing alone. Did anything happen——?'

But before answering him Donna had to absorb what lay in the meaning of his words —that Serafina couldn't sleep and wanted coffee. It implied an intimacy Donna had tried to avoid facing . . . it meant that Rick had been with Serafina during the night. Pain seemed to grab hold of her heart and she had to make an effort not to jerk away from his hand as it held her by the wrist.

'Something has happened,' he said grimly. 'Come, tell me!'

She did so and became a little choked up for more than one reason when she came to the part about Adone not wishing her to phone his mother in case she became upset. 'She was with you!' Donna wanted to cry out. 'She had your arms around her!'

'To drive like that with a passenger!' Rick exclaimed. 'He could have hurt you! You are all right, eh? In one piece?'

Donna felt the touch of his hands and this time she did jerk away from him. 'I—I'm perfectly all right,' she said stiffly. 'I had my safety-belt fastened, and Adone would have been all right had he fastened his. He was driving like that because of the argument he had with you!'

'So you heard.' Rick thrust a cigarette between his lips and there was an impatient click-click of his lighter as he applied the flame. 'He takes advantage of Serafina's generosity to him—you are helping her to write this book, so you must realise how hard she worked to make her money. Do you think it right that a man of Adone's age should sponge on his mother and make no attempt to find an occupation for himself? So he didn't whimper at a little pain! Is that supposed to prove that he's a man? He has a strain of something in him that I don't like and never will—he takes advantage of women! They are prey to him!'

Donna shivered, for it seemed terrible to her to hear Rick speaking like this of Adone, who was part of his own bloodstream; whose very bone-structure proclaimed him part of this man who spoke so angrily that the cigarette smoke gave the illusion of scorching words.

'He's been hurt,' she said huskily. 'Can't you feel a little sympathy for him?'

'It is Serafina who will need the sympathy when she hears that the young fool has injured that classical face of his.' Smoke gushed from Rick's lips, and then they twisted into a cynical smile. 'With that face and her flair for drama he could get into Italian movies any time he wished, but he's a lazy young hound. He prefers to chase the women —well, I don't have to tell you, do I? I hope this sensational little accident and the interesting scar won't go to your head. He's flawed in some way. You have to realise it, Donna, for I don't want you to make a ruin of your love life.'

'How can you speak like that about him——?' Donna bit her lip. 'He's Serafina's son, after all, and you care greatly for her.'

'Yes,' Rick agreed. 'I have great caring for her, but love doesn't blind us to the faults we see in those we care for. All the same, a girl like you—you are worth the love of a real man.'

Rick turned away as he said this, straightened to his full height and lifted his gaze to the sky that was becoming tinted like pearl. In that moment Donna couldn't take her eyes from the strength of his face. The passionate face of some dark angel, she thought, who had never really found heaven. What would it be like to be in Serafina's shoes . . . to have him for lover and guardian . . . her whip and caress?

'A new day begins,' he murmured. 'Virgin as you, Donna.'

She felt the colour warm her cheeks and she wondered if he was thinking that he would like to be the man to show her the pleasures and perils of love.

'Has it struck you, Donna, how alone we are right now? In the heart of the mountains, with only the birds and the wild hares to witness that we have each other's company at last.'

Her heart pulsed an excited rhythm it had no right to feel. He was Serafina's and if she had any sense she would ask right now to be driven home to the villa. She glanced across at the dark-blue Impala and the sensible words were on her lips, but the impulse to prolong their aloneness was too strong to be denied.

He turned towards her as if he sensed in her silence her desire not to end this hour alone. He held out a hand to her. 'Come and stretch your legs,' he invited. 'Let's take a little walk.'

Donna didn't argue with him but slid from the Maserati and joined him, feeling his warm strong hand enclose hers. They mounted the slope at the side of the road, crushing the herbs and grasses under their feet. The scent of them arose in the fresh air and the early wind combed the hair from her brow. They walked in silence, but she knew they were both aware of the current of physical attraction running from his fingers straight into her veins. It was tingling, electrical, leading them in among the peaceful trees where the birds piped and the butterflies darted in the vagrant streams of light. Now and again Rick glanced down at her with a faint smile of conspiracy, as if he had something in mind that she mustn't ask about. Her answering smile was slightly grave, and she knew she felt more guilty than he about this stolen hour with him. Her hair was tumbled about her shoulders in soft disarray and each time he looked at her it was as if a slim flame burned in her body. She noticed that the belt of his trench coat was twisted, proof of how hurriedly he had flung it on over a high-necked black sweater and black trousers.

'This is how two people should walk together,' he said. 'Not talking too much but absorbing the enjoyment of each other. You wanted this as much as I did . . . I can feel it.'

It was exciting that Rick should want to be alone with her, but always like the throb of a bruise, persistent through the pleasure, was his relationship to Serafina. He made no secret of the need La Neri had of him, and when he was with her it was plain to anyone watching them that his devotion was unstinting. But there was another side to Rick and he seemed to reveal it only when he and Donna were able to snatch a little time together.

The toughness seemed to melt away a little and he made her aware that he could be tender. It was as if he found with her a little of the youth he had lost during those years he had searched for his mother's killer . . . a breath of innocence he had to snatch, as if sometimes he became stifled by the exotic presence of Serafina, the sophistication, the mannerisms, the beauty he knew so well.

All at once the trees where they walked seemed to grow less dense and as the daylight cleared away the shadows they came upon the strangest little building Donna had ever seen in her life . . . strange and yet delightful, its walls completely covered with climbing plants. 'It's called a *trullo sovrano,*' Rick told her, as they paused to look at it. 'They aren't usually seen in this part of Italy, but I had it built so it was an exact copy of those little houses. It is a house, you know. My den—my secret hide-away.'

Donna gazed at it in fascination, a two-storied, circular stone house with a cone-shaped roof of small tiles beautifully laid so that they overlapped. It was rectangular in shape with narrow windows and an oval-shaped door.

'Would you like to see the inside?' Rick

asked, and he gave her a smile that slumbered in his eyes, half-humorously, as if he were aware of the nervousness at war with her eagerness to step in through that door with him and shut the world outside. As she gripped his hand she could feel with her thumb the tiny hairs on the backs of his fingers and there swept over her the awareness that he was completely male and not entirely governed by conventional behaviour.

'I'm not going to make mad, passionate love to you,' he drawled. 'I did think of making us some breakfast.'

She smiled but couldn't prevent the dash of wild colour across her cheekbones. 'Is the house really yours,' she asked, 'and do you come here often?'

'Not as often as I'd like.' Somehow a significant remark, as if Serafina's demands on him weren't always welcome. He led Donna to the door of the *trullo sovrano* and unlocked it with a little key that he took from his pocket; a key on a chain with a charm she couldn't help noticing, for it was a camel carved from a piece of polished amber.

Catching her glance upon it Rick explained that it had been given to him a long time ago by an old Sicilian woman who originated from a half-wild region in the desert. 'I was a bit of a boy then,' he said. 'She told me that because the camel has such patience and endurance he is the only infidel admitted into

132

paradise. I've carried the charm ever since—heaven knows why! Would you like to have it, Donna?'

'Indeed not, Rick.' She gave him a slightly shocked look. 'It might bring you bad luck to give away a charm you've had all these years. I was admiring its prettiness, that's all.'

'Don't you get the urge to possess what you admire?' Rick murmured, and he captured her gaze before she could look away from him.

'Not when I know that it belongs to someone else,' she said quietly.

His eyes held hers, then his eyebrow quirked to let her know he took her meaning and he returned the charm to his pocket and pushed open the door of the cone-roofed house. He moved his hand in a gesture of invitation and Donna tried to look casual as she entered what Rick had called his hideaway. It was a word that implied secrecy and she couldn't help but wonder if he ever brought other women here, and aware that he might read the question in her eyes she concentrated on looking round the main room, with thick white walls and the windows deepset above an alcove with a couch. She saw that the window-frames were carved with strange birds and animals, and on the deep sills were a pair of lovely old water jars. There was a table and a pair of chairs and a colourful rug covered the stone floor. A small spiral stairway led to the upper room, which Donna guessed was a replica of this room, only it probably contained a bed.

'What are you thinking?' Rick asked, and throwing off his trench coat he approached another alcove in which stood a small stove, with a sink and a cupboard.

'I don't quite know what to think,' she said. 'This is all so different from the villa—it's all so very simple, and I never thought of you as a man who went in for simplicity.'

'Each one of us is a divided creature,' he said, opening the cupboard and taking from it a packet of spaghetti, a can of tomatoes and a pan. 'I relish being able to step beneath a shower each morning, but I also enjoy cooking spaghetti for myself—and sometimes for a guest.'

'Do you often invite people to your hideaway?' She spoke casually and stood looking at the titles of books on a carved shelf.

'You mean women, eh?' He spoke with equal casualness as he turned a tap and water filled the pan, though Donna would have sworn the place wasn't actually plumbed. He caught the look she threw at him and gestured at the windows. 'I have a tank outside which is filled from a nearby stream. Carrying the water from the stream represents something of a task, but when I use my den and I'm able to make coffee for myself, then I'm glad I took the trouble. I don't use this place for carrying on love affairs, if you were wondering.'

'I wasn't——'

'Of course you were.' He lit the stove and a blue flame flared under the pan of water. 'It's a natural reaction. Why else, you wonder, would a man want to build a place like this, hidden away among the trees, with only the birds and bees for neighbours? Would you believe that I sometimes wish to be on my own?'

Donna's fingers clenched on a book she had taken down from the shelf, which was beautifully illustrated with all sorts of birds. Her glance moved around this white-walled, alcoved room with its gothic windows and floor of dark tiles . . . yes, tiles, not stones as she had first assumed.

'Did you build this house yourself?' she asked, a catch in her voice. 'Did you lay the tiles on the roof and the floor, and do all that carving around the window frames? Did you, Rick?'

'You like it all the better for knowing that?' He put spaghetti into the steaming pan. 'Did you imagine that all I could do was play poker and look tough? I was brought up in Sicily where boys are taught to be men at an early age. I was taught carpentry and bricklaying by my father, and by my mother I was shown how to use a chisel on wood. She had magic in her fingers where I have only a painstaking adequacy—the Mafia killed her

135

with the chisel she used for her work.'

'Oh, God!' Donna felt the blood leave her face.

He scowled blackly, a can opener poised above the canned tomatoes as if it would have given him satisfaction to have used it as a weapon on the man he had eventually killed with his hands. 'Childhood makes us, so it's said. It made me in one black hour, and after that I was full grown in my heart even if my body was still a boy's, and there was no more playtime. They left my mother dead, but my——'

He stopped there, abruptly, and opened the can of tomatoes with a quick, strong twist of his hand. 'How do you prefer your spaghetti, salty or bland?'

'I—I'll leave it to you.' Donna was staring at him, aching to hear more about that terrible time in his life, instinctively aware that he didn't often talk about it.

'Adone has told you things about me, eh?' he said. 'I guessed he had from the way you sometimes look at me.'

'How do I look at you?' she asked.

'Like a half-frightened girl, and like a woman who cares that a boy had his heart broken.'

'Oh, my dear——'And there it was her turn to break off, as if she had said too much and yet not enough.

He shrugged, drained the pan of spaghetti

and tipped it into a dish and placed the dish in the warming compartment of the stove. Butter sizzled in the frying pan while he drained off excess juice from the tomatoes and tipped them into the hot butter. All his movements, Donna noticed, had economy and purpose about them, and it felt good to watch him and to know that she was someone with whom he could find sympathy and relaxation. She felt certain that with Serafina he rarely talked of his past, nor did he bring her to his *trullo sovrano* to eat the kind of meal he would often have enjoyed in his mother's kitchen.

Donna curled down on his couch with the book of birds, but her eyes were upon Rick as he percolated coffee and opened a small tin of Nestlé's milk. She knew that she was sharing something special with him; something they would have to pretend had never happened when they were back together under Serafina's roof. That was the hemlock in his intoxicating wine . . . La Neri's hold on him.

She breathed the tang of herbs as he gave a pinch to the tomatoes and the aroma mingled with the hot coffee, and Donna wished ardently that this hour could never end, that each and every day she might be alone like this with Rick, and that when the day drew to its close and the night settled over the roof he had made strong and lovely, his arms might close strong around her and hold her with loving against the heart she had healed with her love.

As her heart confessed in silence her love for him, he brought food to the table and beckoned her to come and eat. He laughed at the ungainly way she ate her spaghetti and showed her the trick of winding it on the fork, rich with butter, herbs and tomatoes.

'Good?' he smiled, a deep crevice in his dark cheek. 'I've often thought I could make a good thing of my own *trattoria.*'

'Why not, Rick?' she asked, hands clasped about her cup of coffee. 'I could be your waitress.'

He flung back his head and laughed, and never before had she heard him laugh like that. 'I believe you mean it, little one, but I am too much the Sicilian to expose your charms to the pinching fingers of Italian customers.'

Donna felt the colour move in her cheeks, for she didn't miss the way Rick ran his eyes over her, nor the deepening note in his voice, as if he thought there were delicious aspects to her.

'You love Sicily very much, don't you?' she said, lashes half-lowered as she twined spaghetti around her fork. 'Do you go there sometimes?'

'I would be a dead man if I did so,' he said ironically.

Donna gave him a shocked look and he

inclined his head. 'There is a hunk of stone in Sicily with my name carved upon it. I have enemies.' He snapped his fingers in a significant way. 'It happens if you cross the brotherhood, and I have done so, on more than one occasion.'

'Are you safe—here?' she asked, and her lashes had lifted to expose the anxiety in her eyes.

'Let us say I am safer.' He lifted the coffee pot and refilled their cups. 'It is all right, Donna, there is no need to look as if they are going to crash in here with their guns blazing. They hate me, but they respect me at the same time, and the days have passed when they could kill in Italy without the hammer of justice coming down on their heads. But Sicily is still rather untamed, and that is one of the reasons why I love it. I might indeed have taken the chance of seeing my old home again, but I have—responsibilities.'

He meant Serafina . . . it was there in his face that grew brooding as he leaned back in his chair and drank his coffee. Yes, thought Donna, she would be terrified of letting Rick go home to the island where death might stalk him in the hot sunlight or the dark shadows. Rick was the rock on which Serafina had built her life and she was never going to let go of him.

'I'll wash the dishes,' Donna said, jumping to her feet. 'You smoke a cigarette—I know

139

you're longing for one.'

'What if I said, Donna, that I was longing for you?'

There was a silence and she didn't dare to look at him. 'Have you any washing-up liquid for the pans?' she asked, forcing a calmness into her voice which her heart was far from feeling.

'The dishes can wait.' His chair moved as he stood up, and because she didn't dare to be taken unaware by him Donna swung round to face him. He came towards her, graceful as a lean panther, looking as if those deep, dark elements in his life had cast their shadows into his very flesh. His eyes pinned her on their dark steel. 'I know,' he said, almost grimly. 'I know I promised not to touch you, but I've got to. Just this once I want to pretend that you are mine.' His voice became raw, savage. 'I want you near to me! I want what I can never have beyond this moment!'

She saw his eyes smouldering darkly above her and then he plucked her to him and his hand wrapped itself about her throat as if it were a stem he could snap . . . if she dared to defy him. She didn't even want to. Her slimness, her youth, were lost in his embrace and his head was clasped by her hands as he caressed her throat with his lips and then slowly brought them to her mouth, capturing the soft little cry she gave.

The power and strength in his kiss . . . the

piercing sweet demand . . . these were not the lightly given caresses of a man amusing himself for a while. Donna knew it with all her being, folded closer to Rick than she had ever been to anyone, body and limbs crushed to his as if he wanted to melt her into himself. With the movement of his lips came the fiery little words she couldn't understand but which she knew originated from his native island. His hands brushed themselves through her hair, cradled her nape, came down over her shoulders, hard in themselves and yet with tenderness in their tips. His mouth moved against hers until with a breathless gasp she buried her face in the warmth of his throat. Her eyes came slowly open to meet his, drugged from the power of his kisses.

Those deep, searching, unrelenting kisses which had ravished her inmost heart, so that now he must know her secret.

'We kiss and make exciting vibrations, eh?' he murmured. 'There is no shame in it, a man and a woman should feel like this with each other, as if they have no need of anything but a place to be alone together. I want to know, have you ever kissed like that with anyone else?'

She shook her head and felt the cashmere of his sweater against her cheek, and the long hard pressure of his legs against hers. His hand stroked across her hair as if he loved the soft feel of it. 'I wouldn't change one hair of your head,' he said. 'I wouldn't change you in any way, and I wish you could stay always the young, pure, so sweet to hold English girl. I think I would like to put you in a nunnery because I can't have you.'

Donna pressed her fingers against the back of his neck, where it was warm and so curiously vulnerable, so different from the rest of him that felt so hard. She could say it now and what they both wanted could happen, up there in the soft shadowy room into which the little staircase twined. Her heart beat like a soft drum and she was about to say the word when his hand closed gently over her mouth.

'Let it be good like this,' he murmured. 'Even though it would be wonderful for me to carry you up those stairs. Just to know that you would like it, Donna, lights up a flame inside me. But there is always the reality to face afterwards.' He cupped her face in his hands and gazed down into her eyes. 'We both have dreams, but mine are snared and cannot be set free. You understand me, don't you? You aren't a girl that a man takes lightly . . . you are a girl that he takes for always or not at all.'

He smiled a little and bent to brush her lips with his. 'Ah yes, you would be generous for the sake of that boy . . . that Sicilian boy of long ago who came home to find death in his house.'

'Oh—Rick!' Her mouth moved under his

and once again he gathered her close to him in hard hunger that he refused to satisfy for her sake. Her lips and hands clung to him and for a short while, there in his arms, there was no tomorrow, and no woman named Serafina to hold out elegant hands that had a grip on Rick no other woman could hope to break. It was Rick who with a sudden groan put Donna away from him.

He turned from her and went to where he had flung his trench coat. He sought in the pockets and took out a pack of cigarettes, ripping them open with his thumb. Came the click of his lighter and smoke wreathed about his dark head. There was a silence that in itself was a kind of desolation.

He moved to a window and Donna watched him, his strong profile against the light, faintly frowning, the cigarette fixed to his lip. 'Sometimes the right people meet at the wrong time,' he said broodingly. 'That night on the steps of the Colosseum we were strangers and yet we knew each other. Later on when we danced I think if I suggested to you that we run away together you would have come with me without asking a single question. Am I right?'

'I might have asked if I could fetch my overnight bag,' she said, the smile shaky on her mouth.

'So easy to do,' he said gravely. 'To chase the rainbow, to get lost among its soft golds and shining curves, and to hell with the past because every man is entitled to some kind of a dream. But it wouldn't have worked . . . I was even tempted that night on the terrace to warn you against coming to work at the villa. We were attracted to each other, but I should have told you then and there that I wasn't free to do anything about it. Not then, Donna. Not now—or ever.'

'I understand, Rick——'

'Do you?' He swung to face her and a ribbon of blue smoke twisted from his lips. 'Tell me what you understand.'

'That loyalty means more to you than —love.'

'Love passes, child, when it has to—when the thrill wears off!'

'No——' Her hand was held out to him in mute appeal.

'It does, Donna, when it can't be satisfied in the way that nature meant it to be. Love isn't all romance and sweet wild words. It's a hunger and a craving that feed on themselves if the body has to be denied. In the end all that is left is the bitterness, the dregs. You have the sweet wine of youth in your veins, *carina*. Your life and loving are ahead of you.'

'You're being cruel——'

'To be kind.'

There seemed no answer to that and no chance, Donna felt it stabbingly, to be happy with him, free to roam where they would, to hold hands in candlelit restaurants, to wander through art galleries and old Italian churches, things she would have loved to do with Rick because now she had been shown the secret side of him . . . the side he didn't show to those who thought of him as the tough body-guard of Serafina Neri.

'I know what you are thinking,' he said, and there was something of carved Italian stone about him, an obdurate power in his face and body that made Donna want to run to him and pound against the wall that kept her out of his inmost heart. It wasn't that she wanted to possess him . . . she so desperately longed to be part of him.

'Are all my thoughts so transparent to you?' She couldn't keep the hurt note out of her voice, for she had just learned that loving someone brought with it a special kind of pain and sensitivity.

'In this instance the current of your thoughts is like a live wire I am touching.' The black sweater was high against his throat, lending shadow to his features. 'You want me to lay it all bare, what holds me to Serafina. You feel you have the right to know and you're asking yourself is it because she's a rich woman. It isn't! Sufficient to say that I have to put her before you, this woman whom others think of as the sex tigress she portrayed in her films. I know the reality of her and that I have it within my power to break her heart. I won't do it, Donna. I won't let you be part of another woman's heartbreak. I won't flaw in any way the sweet goodness I find in you, the tender kindness in your mind and body. I know I make you suffer when I speak like this, but imagine that suffering in someone older, a woman who on the outside appears to have everything, yet who is really the victim of fears you can have no conception of.'

He fell silent a moment, his shoulders hard and firm as he stood with the light from the window behind him so his face was masked in shadows.

'I think you can imagine what would happen to that woman if I left her to find a little of my lost youth with a young girl. I think you know what would happen to us if we had to live with that knowledge.' He drew a harsh breath. 'I—I can't find it in me to rape that woman's feelings.'

Donna winced at the word he used . . . a terrible word that induced a graphic image of the proud and beautiful Serafina flung down in wounded disarray, weeping among the shards of her broken heart.

No, thought Donna, it wasn't in Rick to be that cruel, and battling with her tears she turned blindly to the sink and began to wash the dishes. She heard the click of Rick's lighter and breathed the drifting cigarette smoke. He smoked far too much, as if he had tensions which had to find a certain relief.

Suddenly Donna couldn't endure losing him completely, and with her hands dripping water and suds she swung to face him. 'Why should I be coy?' she said tensely. 'I realise that you and I have no future together, but that doesn't mean we can't—after all, we don't have to hurt anyone. Rick, I want to know what it feels like to be with you—really with you, just this once.'

His nostrils tensed and the tip of his cigarette glowed bright as he drew the smoke deep into his lungs. 'The hell you do!' The words whipped from his mouth. 'Do you think that's all you mean to me? Someone to take to bed for an illicit hour, like some harlot who is nothing more than a willing body to please mine? If that's all you meant to me, then I should have carried you up those stairs an hour ago. I'm only human! I enjoy having a woman in my arms—and to have you——

'*Cristo dio,*' he raked a hand through his hair until it sprawled black across his brow, 'don't ask me to treat you like that! I could, heaven help me, but with every decent impulse in me I don't want to. I want to cherish what we have, Donna. I want to remember it as something good and sweet, my heart.'

'But it feels so lonely, Rick, being good and sweet.' She came to him and lifted a hand to the lines in his face, which seemed to have deepened as if he were making an effort not to reach out for her. 'Didn't you mean it when you said that one night the black knight might climb in through my balcony? I wouldn't scream, Rick.'

'I was teasing you when I said that.'

'Were you, Rick?' Her hand slid up the front of his sweater. 'And are you pretending to breathe so unevenly, or is it all that smoking?'

'I warn you not to try me too far, Donna. I'm not made of stone.'

'No, Rick, you're warm brown flesh and wide shoulders, and when I touch you I feel as if my legs are going to give way. If you put me up on a pedestal I shall promptly fall off.'

'Little devil!' He caught her gently by the hair and looked down into her eyes, seeing there the candour and yearning she made no effort to hide. 'You wouldn't be able to do this with a younger man, so don't you ever try it on.'

'You mean he wouldn't have your cast-iron control, is that it, Rick?' She pulled away from him, hurting the roots of her hair. 'Sorry to fling myself at you, but I didn't realise I was dealing with someone so noble.'

'I'm older than you, and wiser,' he grated. 'It never ends with just one stolen hour . . . if I swept you off your feet and carried you up into that cool little room, soft with shadow, do you really imagine it could end there? We'd want more . . . enough for a thousand days and nights. I refuse to risk it!'

'There's no need to sound so emphatic, Rick.' She gave him a smile and was determined not to let him see that his rejection hurt so very much. 'Why should you risk your position at the villa for the sake of a little nobody like me? You can rest assured that in future I shall be a little wiser, and not mistake a few kisses for the sign of something more significant. You'll have to put it down to my crass inexperience in these matters.'

'I put it down to your romantic young heart.' He gestured at the sink where the dishes were still swimming about in the water. 'I'd be grateful if you would carry on with the washing up. I gather someone has to go down and pick up the invalid and I think it had better be me than Adone's mother. I'll leave my key with you, Donna, so you can lock up the house when you leave—you will easily find your way to the villa if you follow the path that leads away from the rear of the *trullo sovrano*.'

Rick turned and picked up his trench coat, swinging it like a cloak about his shoulders. His cigarette jutted from the corner of his mouth and his eyes were narrowed against the updrifting smoke, towards his hair that was still rumpled. Two-faced Janus, Donna told herself, keeper of the gate of another woman's heart.

He strode to the door and opened it and there he glanced back at her. For a brief moment he just looked at her and she despised the way she melted just to see that strong Latin face and commanding air, and that something just a little wicked about him . . . a wickedness that right now was offset by a deep glint of humour in his eyes, half-wistful.

'*Arrivederci, mia.* Don't think I wouldn't like to be the one who "*will give thee the treasures of darkness and hidden riches of secret places*".'

Then he was gone, striding away from her, and with a little bleak smile she turned her attention to the plates and pans. When she had finished and tidied them away a quietness fell over the house and Donna stood there looking about her and feeling a sudden sense of loneliness. Her gaze rested on the little staircase that twined its way to the upper regions and she realised that she couldn't leave without seeing that cool, softly shadowed room, as Rick had called it.

The little twining stairway was soon mounted and the room above was white-walled and peaceful as the cell of a monk. The divan bed was covered by a simple woven quilt and above it on the wall was a painting of old castle ruins lying scattered on a hill, half buried in wild flowers. On a small carved table beside the bed was a small oil-lamp . . . and also a woman's picture in a plain gold frame.

With a sudden tremor in her hand Donna picked up the framed picture and studied it . . . the woman was lovely and in a very serene fashion, with dark hair drawn away and simply styled about her face. It was the depth and darkness of the eyes that told Donna who she was, and there swept over her a feeling of acute pity bordering on terror. She glanced over her shoulder as if someone had come into the room, but htere were only the corner shadows into which the light from the small windows didn't reach. Donna felt her wrist shaking and replaced the picture on the table in fear of dropping it.

Rick's mother . . . and perhaps the real reason why he wouldn't bring a woman to this room in order to make love to her. Donna stroked a hand across the single, white-covered pillow, and there was a sweet hollow aching deep in her bones. Only now, only in this moment, did Rick truly belong to her. Into this moment was packed all the sweetness that might have been, all the bitterness of what could never be.

And it was then that she caught sight of a small carved box just behind the lamp and she couldn't resist the impulse to lift the lid and have one more glimpse into what was private to Rick. Inside the box lay a pair of masks;

151

one was black and the other one was silver, and Donna remembered a pair of eyes smiling at her through the slits of the black mask, and the touch of lean fingers peeling the silver mask from her face there on that dawn-lit terrace above the city of Rome.

So he had kept the masks just as she had kept the rose . . . wanting to remember the way they had met . . . needing to keep something for when they must part.

She gently closed the box, and a few minutes later had locked the house and was making her way back to the Villa Imperatore, where she must behave towards Rick like a polite stranger and never let it show that she knew what it felt like when he took a woman in his arms and let his warm, demanding lips rove her skin.

Donna drew her little velvet jacket around her . . . Rick had kissed her and then he had put her out of his arms, and at the villa there was never to be any escape from seeing him with the woman he had chosen to keep in his arms.

From now on it would take all Donna's endurance to carry on working for Serafina, but she had signed a contract and couldn't break it without damaging her career as a freelance secretary. She was bound to stay at the villa until the memoirs were completed, and so far La Neri was only halfway through the book.

She came in sight of the villa, but it no longer struck her as beautiful . . . now it seemed like a prison in which she must serve a sentence that would be exquisitely painful.

Chapter Seven

For about the tenth time Serafina took hold of her son's photograph and studied it. 'He was so handsome when this was taken a year ago,' she mourned. 'That scar on his lip has altered him, Donna. It has given him a look of—of menace.'

'Not really.' Donna sat in a chair beside the daybed on which her employer was attractively arranged in flower-printed shantung with full sleeves; a notebook was open in Donna's hand and her pen was poised, but they weren't getting very far with the new chapter.

'Why do you say not really, when I have only to compare him scarred with this picture in which he has no blemish at all?' Serafina gave her secretary a frowning look. 'I know him better than you, so don't argue with me.'

'I'm not arguing,' Donna said reasonably. 'It's only that he had a fuller lower lip before the accident and now the scar has tightened it and slightly altered his expression. Apart from that he is still a remarkably good-looking man.'

'Man—yes, that is it.' Serafina pounced on the word. 'That is what has happened, and suddenly I realise that my Adone is a man and no longer a charming, feckless boy. Was he in great pain when it happened, Donna? And was he very brave about having to be stitched without the anaesthetic?'

'Very brave,' Donna assured her, for about the dozenth time. 'The scar would have been more noticeable because the ether would have relaxed the facial muscles and made the stitching more difficult. He really hasn't lost his attractiveness, Serafina. In fact——' Donna paused, for in her opinion that loss of sensuality in Adone's lower lip had somehow improved him, and it was noticeable that when he smiled his mouth took a slightly twisted look that intensified his resemblance to Rick.

Serafina leaned back against a silk pillow and studied Donna with narrowed eyes that were clear jade in her magnolia face, whose skin was kept supple with expensive lotions and massage and a rigorous diet from which she never strayed. 'You find my son attractive, don't you?' she said in a silken tone of voice, her eyes running over the slim lines of Donna's figure in a simple belted dress with short sleeves. Since living under the warm Italian sun her skin had taken on a honey-hued tan which set off the natural fairness of her hair, recently re-styled into a pageboy with a smooth undercurl.

'Any girl with normal eyesight and natural instincts would find Adone attractive,' Donna smiled, for it was both a shield and a source of danger hiding behind Adone's unconcealed interest in her. His mother was well aware that they swam together in the big green-tiled pool and lazed in the sun at the poolside. Since his accident Adone had been less prone to fast driving and gambling and had taken to enjoying the amenities of his own home. Apart from the swimming-pool there was a games room fitted out with a large snooker table, another for ping-pong, a dart-board and even a one-armed bandit which had been smuggled into the villa by Rick because Serafina found it amusing. Being a gambling machine it was illegal on private premises, but Donna had already learned the painful way that Rick would go to quite a few lengths to keep La Neri happy.

There was also a projection room at the villa and it was fun to watch the old movies in which Serafina had starred, and also quite a few others made by the stars of the golden era of Hollywood. Seated in the velvety gloom of that small cinema with its comfortable arm-chairs, and potently aware of Rick's drifting cigarette smoke, Donna had to admit that her prison was a luxurious one. But the subtle torment of being so near to Rick and yet so apart from him had a way of building up and creating a tension that sometimes kept her awake for hours. She would find herself tossing and turning in bed, her mind tortuously alive with images of him alone with Serafina. Each morning if there wasn't a reel of dictation on the tape-recorder she would feel the hot agony of jealous reproach . . . how could she love a man whose body and soul were so in bondage to the demands of another woman?

This very morning Serafina had sent for her to come and take notes because the tape-recorder had not been employed last night, and Donna felt a twisting pain inside her each time she noticed the faint mauve shadows under Serafina's eyes, and directly she had entered the rose and ivory *sala* attached to the big bedroom Donna had breathed the tang of Rick's cigarettes.

'Adone finds you equally attractive, does he not?' Serafina moved a plush buffer across the shining surfaces of her long fingernails.

'It's only because we're thrown together quite a lot,' Donna said, a trifle defensively. 'I—I don't want you to imagine that I'm getting any foolish notions about him. I'm your secretary and I'm grateful that you allow me to enjoy the amenities of your house.'

'There is no need to sound so prickly.' Serafina gave a low, purring laugh. 'I know my son and I don't want you to be hurt by him—he has hurt others with his careless philandering, but most of them were women who should have known better than to get into his clutches. I—well, I agree with Rick that you are a different type of young woman. You haven't played around with men, have you?'

'I've never felt like doing so.' The uncontrollable colour had come into Donna's cheeks at Serafina's mention of Rick ... so they discussed her, and he had evidently dropped the hint that Adone was becoming a little too attentive. Donna was torn between the thrill of knowing he cared what became of her, and a dash of resentment that he should interfere in her private life.

Serafina's eyes followed that flow of colour and the way it dwelt on Donna's cheekbones, and a gleam of speculation came into her green eyes. 'Ah, is it possible you are in love, Donna? You blush like a girl whose heart is beating a little too fast—ah yes, it is all too possible! My Adone has the charm of the devil himself, and you are young and inexperienced. My child, I hope he hasn't seduced you?'

'Of course not——'

'You are English and reserved, and that would appeal to Adone after the easy way he has conquered women of the more willing sort. You are as well so much his opposite in a physical sense, so fair, and so charmingly restrained in the white bathing suit that you wear when you swim with my son.' Serafina reached out and touched with an elegant finger the slim watch-strap on Donna's wrist. 'Has he mentioned that he is betrothed to an Italian girl who is completing her education at the Convent of the Lilies in Florence?'

Strangely enough Donna was neither surprised by Adone's engagement, nor in the least concerned that he hadn't told her about it himself. Such a revelation would hardly have been conducive to a flirtation with her, but even as she looked politely interested it was evident from the way Serafina was regarding her that she had expected a more emotional reaction to the news.

'I suppose you imagined that your blonde attractions would overcome my son's sense of duty where this other girl is concerned?' The velvety tones had hardened. 'From your lack of surprise you must have known that he had made an agreement to marry in the near future.'

'I had no idea he was engaged, but I'm not altogether surprised.' Donna tried not to sound cynical. 'I do realise that in Latin countries it is still in practice for the parents of a girl to engage her to a man before she is barely out of the schoolroom.'

'Isabeta will complete her education quite soon, and then the arrangements for the marriage will be made. I wanted you to know where you stood with my son. I didn't want you to get the idea that he was free to become seriously involved with you. Adone is aware that I wish to see him wedded to a young Italian girl in the old way of our country.'

There was a pause and the long-nailed fingers patted Donna's hand as if in consolation. 'You must accept, my dear, that you are just an interlude in my son's life, a means of distraction for a virile young man who will settle down as soon as he's married. Isabeta is a sweet child and she will make him a nice young wife. She is what I want for him, you understand?'

'Yes,' said Donna, who understood perfectly that Serafina was making possessively sure that Adone's prospective wife didn't steal him away from her. She meant to bind Adone to her just as she had bound Rick; neither of the men closest to her was ever going to be set free of her seductive coils.

'So you are not the sort to make a scene,' Serafina purred. 'The British are very self-contained, aren't they? Pride comes before passion, eh? We Latins are much more volatile and I am sure it is for the best that we marry our own sort. Adone's young bride will make him happy.'

Donna felt quite sure that a young and obedient girl straight out of a convent would have little chance of exerting her own character and claims in the house of La Neri. Doubtless the couple would live here, where Adone could have access to his mother's cheque-book and continue to be spoiled until he lost the charm and courage that might have helped him to overcome his self-indulgent ways.

When a sigh escaped Donna it was immediately pounced on by Serafina. 'I am sorry, my dear, if I have hurt and disappointed you, but it's best for you to be in the picture.' She gave a throaty laugh. 'My little pun, you understand.'

She leaned back against her silk pillows, curving her arms about her head so that the shantung sleeves fell away seductively from her bare arms. One of them wore a wide gold slave-bracelet, but this woman was no man's slave, Donna told herself. She was the one who did the enslaving, and who could blame any man in full command of his instincts for responding to such a woman? Despite the intermittent gleam of silver in her hair, it was still rich and abundant about her elegant neck and lovely, striking face. She stretched her shapely body with a hint of voluptuousness and once again Donna took note of those interesting shadows beneath the jade-coloured eyes.

Donna felt again that stab of sheer pain, so physical that she had to hold her breath in case she actually groaned with it. She could hardly bear it that Rick belonged to this woman who lived only to please herself. It was there in every line of her body, so carefully preserved that she still had the curves and the provocation of ageless desirability. Her skin was as supple as silk beneath the shantung gown, and those mauve shadows that mingled with the green of her eyes gave to her face a look of sensual exhaustion.

'So now we understand each other,' Serafina drawled. 'You will not lose your heart to Adone if you're a wise girl, though I suppose I can't stop him from encouraging you to lose your—head. Anyway, you are English and emancipated and it has to happen some time to most women. I imagine my Adone is an excellent lover . . . perhaps even a little ruthless, if one is to believe in hereditary impulse.'

Donna felt the quickening of her pulses . . . Serafina was referring in a subtle way to Adone's paternity, and Donna could well believe that he had inherited a certain ruthlessness from Rick. She moved restlessly and the notebook fell from her knee and sprawled open on the thick carpet of tawny velvet. She bent to pick it up and when she straightened she avoided Serafina's eyes and moved her gaze about this lovely *sala,* with its gilt-scrolled wall panels, beautifully draped silver-white curtains, crystal wall lamps in clusters, and ornaments in white jade and onyx. A room straight out of a glamorous film in which La Neri might have starred.

'I don't feel like working today.' Serafina gave a delicate yawn and glanced at her watch on a gold strap, its jasper face surrounded by small glittering diamonds. Each time she moved a fragrant perfume wafted from her, mingling in Donna's nostrils with that lingering tang of cigarette smoke.

'It's almost eleven o'clock and you might as well go and have your coffee and cookies. Yes, run along. We'll start that new chapter in the morning—go and amuse my son, but remember our little talk, won't you?'

'I shan't forget it,' Donna promised, and rose to her feet. She felt tense, but not on account of Adone's engagement. She well knew the reason as she made her escape from Serafina's scented and languid presence. There wasn't a shadow of doubt in her mind that Rick had been with Serafina during the night, and though Donna was painfully aware that she had no sort of hold on him, it stabbed at her sensitivity that he spent his nocturnal hours with another woman.

A sensually seductive and fascinating woman who had probably made him forget that he had ever held Donna in his arms and felt from the contact an excitement which had welded them together in long aching kisses. Kisses that made her shiver in retrospect.

Donna went into the office to place her notebook and pen on the desk . . . a stream

163

of sunshine beckoned her to the windows, but she didn't want to be alone with the silent black knight, with his stone hands forever clasped on his sword and his eyes forever cast downwards, and she made her way through an archway that led to one of the brighter patios so hung with flowers and creepers that it was a haunt of birds and honey-bees.

She wanted to be alone, but her wish wasn't to be granted, and she had walked around the huge sweeping branches of a tree before she realised that this part of the garden was already occupied. She came at once to a standstill beneath the golden honeybags of the laburnum, unable to retreat as Rick caught her with his gaze and Adone swung round from the wrought-iron table where they were seated. The two men arose and Donna was obliged to join them, finding when she reached the table that they were drinking red wine and sharing a plate of sandwiches; thick cuts of smoked ham between slices of brown bread.

She felt a fluttering of nerves in the pit of her stomach and failed to be unaffected by the look of Rick in a chalk-striped shirt, casually open against his muscular throat. She felt the piercing scrutiny he gave her through his lashes and she wanted to resent him for his betrayal of those kisses he had seared into her skin and those whispers she had understood with her senses if not with her ears.

'How nice that you come and join us.'

Adone smiled down at her as she took the seat he drew out for her, and she smiled back at him as if she had been longing to see him.

'Your mother was unable to concentrate on the new chapter and I was told to run away and have my elevenses.' And then, as if devil-driven, Donna glanced at Rick, but his dark, weathered face gave nothing away. He looked his sardonic self, strong and assured in his maleness, with perhaps an extra dash of gravel in his voice when he said to her: 'You must have some wine with us. Perhaps Adone will be gallant enough to fetch an extra wine glass —you will do that, *compare?*'

'Instantly.' Adone drew his fingertips along Donna's bare arm. 'A moment ago, by that tree, you looked as if you had walked out of the cloister of a nun's garden. The pale dress, perhaps, or something in your eyes. You will stay and not run away from Rick, eh? I think he alarms you a little.'

'What nonsense!' she exclaimed. 'I do assure you, Adone, that my nerves are per-fectly steady—Signor Lordetti is only a man, after all. I'm sure he has chinks in his armour like everyone else, despite his tough reputa-tion.'

'At last,' Adone laughed, 'a brave girl who refuses to let the Lordetti legend go to her knees! I will be but a few minutes fetching the wineglass.'

He sauntered away and Donna deliberately

watched him out of sight. She gave an uncontrollable start when fingers lightly touched her wrist, sending an electrical tingle right into her armpit. She drew her hand off the table top into her lap and clenched her fingers together until her fingernails dug into her palm.

'If you flirt with him, he will misunderstand,' Rick drawled.

'Is that what you did?' she asked. 'Do you imagine you're the only man around here whom I find—attractive? I'm English, remember. We're an emancipated race and like the bees and butterflies we flit from one pollen cup to another, getting our wings well dipped in experience.'

'Stop trying to sound like a *demi-mondaine.*' The merest flick of a whip seemed to stir against her skin, making her quiver and look at him defiantly. He leaned there with his glass of wine, but something of him reached out and touched her, though this time he hadn't stirred a finger.

'Stop giving me orders,' she rejoined, letting the resentment into her eyes. 'You haven't got my scalp on your belt, *signore,* even if you think you have.'

'I would love to know why you are talking like a girl who has bitten into a sour lemon.' He took a swig of his wine and gestured at the ham sandwiches. 'Perhaps you are hungry and should eat something.'

'No, thanks.' She looked away from him

and studied a massive wall creeper burdened with bell-flowers and the fluttering wings of big white butterflies.

'Male butterflies attract their mates by carrying perfume on their wings during the time of courtship,' Rick told her. 'A reversal of the human procedure, eh?'

'Oh, I don't know,' Donna rejoined, 'the tang of cigarettes and strong soap can do crazy things to a woman. I imagine we can all get carried away, but thank heaven, we're able to come to our senses—like waking from one of those mad dreams that make no sense and are best forgotten.'

'Was that all it was, sweetheart?' His drawl had become faintly mocking. 'At the time I could have sworn it was an impossible dream from which neither of us wished to awaken.'

'Impossible is the word,' she said tensely. 'I must have been out of my tiny mind to—to let you kiss me.'

'As I recall there was mutual participation, Donna *mia.*' A dangerous little smile had come into his eyes, which held her gaze across the table as if his black pupils were magnetic. 'What has happened to chill the warm ardour I recall so vividly? You were like a rare champagne that went to my head, and now you are bitter lemon with ice. There has to be a reason——'

'Oh yes, Rick, there's a reason,' she broke in, and vivid in her mind was the picture of

Serafina lounging with languid grace on her daybed, the lids of her green eyes weighted with a sensual languor. 'I don't think I have to spell it out, do I? Is your mistress aware that you play games behind her back?'

'My mistress?' He raised an interrogatory eyebrow, and there was a little twist to his mouth that made Donna want to strike it away.

'You know well enough who I mean,' she said coldly.

'You refer to Serafina.' He moved the wine-glass about in his lean fingers and Donna couldn't help but remember the feel of those fingers on her skin, moving with the caressive expertise of a man who knew exactly how to arouse a woman . . . and satisfy her. Only for Donna there could never be sweet satisfaction; in its place there was the aching bitterness of having to live in the house of the woman who had the whole of Rick. It hurt far more than she had imagined it would; it injured her pride as well as her body, for how could she wipe out of her memory that moment when she had offered herself to Rick?

She felt scorched by the memory and couldn't look at him, closing her lashes down over her eyes.

'Aren't you glad now,' he murmured, 'that we didn't take those steps together?'

'Glad to my soul,' she said fiercely. 'At least you had that much conscience!'

'Oh yes, I have a conscience.' He said it with a deep tinge of irony in his voice. 'But few of us can escape the deadly arrow of attraction when it strikes.'

Donna shivered and said involuntarily: 'How painful you make it sound!'

'It is, and we both know it. As if love were only for masochists.'

'Don't talk about—love.' Her eyes blazed their resentment across at him. 'Why couldn't you leave me alone altogether? Why did you have to kiss and pretend——?'

'Pretend, Donna?' He tautened in his seat and his fingers gripped the stem of his wine-glass as if he might break it.

'Weren't you pretending? Playing the Latin lover with the little ninny of a secretary—almost following the script of one of those old films Serafina likes us to watch on her private screen. Is that the way you get your private kicks, Rick? When she lets you off the leash and you go prowling in Rome, do you often come across some little girl lost who lets you——'

'Stop it!' he snarled. 'Another few moments of this and you will be in tears and I shall—control yourself, there's a good girl! Adone is returning, and I have a feeling you are going to need a glass of wine.'

'Here we are.' As Adone arrived at the table Donna managed to do as Rick ordered and was looking fairly composed, though beneath the table her knees were trembling and she was inwardly shaken at how close she had come to losing control. Oh God, it was hell being in love with another woman's lover!

'Serafina is asking for you, Rick,' said Adone, as he poured wine from the jug. 'Something about some accounts she wants you to look at, and a bill which she feels sure she has already paid.'

'I'll go to her.' Rick tossed off the remainder of the wine and rose to his feet, towering a moment beside the table, his tall shadow falling over Donna. She couldn't look at him. She wished to heaven she had never met him!

'A jug of wine and thou, isn't that how it goes?' he drawled, and as he strolled away Donna caught the click of his lighter as he lit a cigarette.

'Lordetti quoting poetry!' Adone gave a laugh as he handed Donna her glass of wine. 'What's got into him, I wonder?'

Donna felt a searching look as Adone sat down beside her and poured wine for himself. Donna remembered the taste, vibrant, just a little sweet, and running warm through the veins . . . the wine Serafina had said her secretary wasn't to drink in working hours, but which she could enjoy right now because she had been given a little holiday.

'Anyway, here's to Signor Lordetti,' she said raising her glass so the sunlight caught in the wine and made it glow a deep ruby.

'What has he done to earn that?' Adone clinked her glass with his, but still there was a searching little light in his eyes.

'Oh,' Donna's smile was bittersweet, 'he left us together, didn't he?'

'So he did.' Adone leaned nearer to her and his eyes softened. 'You do look most ravishingly pretty this morning, *carina*. Your hair reminds me of the pale gold bubbles on a glass of freshly poured champagne, and your skin is like creamy buttermilk with a dash of honey stirred into it. Your mouth is a luscious deep pink, and if I took a bite——'

'Adone,' she said his name with a hint of sweet mockery in her voice, 'should you be saying these things to me? I think you should be saving them for your Latin bride.'

The silence that fell collected into it the chirping of birds, and Donna breathed the pervasive scent of a nearby shrub smothered in white flowers and small redbrown leaves. She sipped her wine and saw Adone's eyes harden into green gems, and the scar became more noticeable as he thinned his lips.

'So that's why you and Lordetti had your heads together when I came into the patio? He was telling you about this girl I'm expected to marry at the end of the summer?'

'It was your mother who told me.' Donna felt a little nervous throb of the heart that he had noticed the atmosphere between herself and Rick. 'She's concerned that you and I might be getting a little too—friendly, but I told her that she has nothing to be worried about. Let me congratulate you on your forthcoming marriage. I understand your *fidanzata* is a nice, sheltered Italian girl from a convent.'

'You imagine I'm in love with this—schoolgirl?' His brows drew together in a disturbingly familiar way, reminding Donna of Rick when he was vexed.

'Love is a usual ingredient in the wedding cake,' she said, with an attempt at lightness. 'Your mother seems happy about her prospective daughter-in-law.'

'She is the only one,' he grunted. 'The last time I saw this girl she had on a pudding hat with a plait under it and I couldn't see her hips for puppy fat. I agreed to the alliance, but I hoped in the meantime that Serafina would forget all about it.'

He touched a finger to his scarred lip and gazed moodily into his wineglass. 'I shall have to call off this ridiculous engagement! *Per dio,* I can't possibly marry someone—what could I possibly want with a naïve girl like that? There is no *amorevolezza,* so how can I stand at the altar and give this girl my vows? For much of the time I have dismissed this *neonata* from my mind, but it would seem that my mother has clung to the idea. Such nonsense! Love is an impulse to embrace, to want someone beyond reason.'

He glanced up suddenly and caught Donna's gaze with his own. 'I shall tell Serafina that I want to marry you!'

Donna could only look at him in speechless shock.

'With you I feel good—desire surges in me when I touch you.'

'That isn't love,' she exclaimed.

'You aren't a schoolgirl, Donna.' His eyes held an eager glow as he leaned towards her. 'You know as well as I that love is mostly physical, with a dash of tolerance and tenderness, and a spicing of the natural conflict between a man and a woman. On my wedding night I want warmth and welcome, not a trembling nun in my arms, who will have been told very little about pleasing a husband. I want fair hair flowing over my pillows like champagne, and your mouth under mine, Donna, all your tantalising reserve melting away as I kiss you until you moan with longing.'

His eyes had kindled and a little nerve pulled at his scarred lip and Donna couldn't help but see in him a haunting likeness to the more hardened man who could shoot love and anguish through her very bones.

'Adone, please stop talking like this. You know as well as I that we can't be anything more than just good friends.' In a kind of desperation she pushed the plate of sandwiches towards him, as if it might provide a barrier. 'Have a ham sandwich and let's change the subject.'

'What humanity you have, *carina.*' He moved his green eyes caressingly over her face. 'You care about the feelings of other people, and you would be amazed how many women care only about themselves, even though they are supposed to be the tender sex. They are obsessed by their looks, and what other people think of them. They go through life believing they are the objects of every man's desire. Even my own mother——' He broke off, shrugged his shoulders eloquently and took a mouthful of wine.

'Serafina is the one who must always be indulged and made happy, even in this matter of my marriage. Tell me something, have you ever noticed that she has scars on her wrists?'

Donna nodded, for she had noticed those wrist scars and had wondered about them. They were fine as hairs but not recent, and Donna couldn't help but suspect that they had been self-inflicted.

Adone inclined his dark head and pushed a strand of hair from his brow, which held a sheen of perspiration. 'It happened about eight years ago, and I believe it had something to do with Rick. They are secretive about their private conflicts, but I suspect that he might have wanted more freedom. He has this club in Rome and a manager to run it, but I imagine he would have liked a more active part in it, but my mother has this constant need of him.'

Adone brooded a moment, running a finger round the rim of his glass. 'How much he loves her I don't really know, but as I say she has this desperate need of him and so in order to punish him for even talking about leaving her, she took a razor blade from his shaver (he has the kind of whiskers that have to be sheared off) and cut her wrists with it. Not pretty, eh? But some women will go to those lengths in order to have their own way.'

He gazed lingeringly at Donna, and she noticed the nervous working of his hand on the table top. 'You would go through hell before you would do that to a man. I feel it in you, this aura of sweet giving and charity. What you are on the outside you are on the inside, and you have no idea how rare that is. I want what you are! I want you!'

He caught hold of her hands, gripping them and pulling them towards him. 'Be mine, Donna. Be my rib, my roots, my woman——'

'No!' She pulled free of his grip and leapt to her feet. 'You can't break your engagement and hurt that girl. In my country it would hardly matter for lots of people there no longer take marriage very seriously, but here in Italy—you know it's still important to keep your word of honour. You know it is!'

'We could go away together, you and I——'

'And what would you do for money?' She just had to say something that would stop all this foolishly romantic talk. 'People work in the real world, Adone, they don't live the lotus life that you do, here at your mother's Shangri-La.'

Adone stared at her, and then it was as if flame had been tossed on to oil—his eyes blazed and Donna saw something awful in them, consuming and dangerous. His look of Rick seemed wiped out and something else was there in its place, and it frightened Donna so that she obeyed wild impulse and fled away from him, across the patio and round the sweep of the lovely old laburnum tree, making for the little inner patio that led into the office.

She heard Adone's chair fall and strike the ground as he leapt to his feet, and she knew she had angered him in a terrible, unexpected way. Her heart pounded as if it were in her throat and even as she ran into the office Adone was at her heels like some infuriated jungle cat. He caught her by the shoulder and spun her around, and his eyes were glittering like a cat's, something primitive and fierce in them.

'Let me go!' She tried to break away from him, but his fingers dug into the bones of her shoulder and made her cry out.

'I'll teach you to throw in my teeth that I live off a woman.' He pulled her roughly to him until he had a tighter grip on her, and then she felt herself half lifted and then flung down painfully on the floor. The next instant Adone was kneeling over her, tangling the fingers of one hand in her hair flung golden across the carpet, while with the other he took a grip on her dress at the neck and ripped it down to her waist. Donna struggled and kicked, but he seemed to have such awful strength, and stark in her mind was something she had once read . . . that a man intent on violating a woman could kill her in his fury and not realise he had done so.

'So you don't care to marry me?' he snarled, his fingers straining at the very roots of her hair. 'You'll be glad to when I've finished with you, you little goody-goody with your haughty ways!'

It was like a nightmare, and the more effort Donna made to escape him the harder and closer this seemed to bring him. 'I beg of you, Adone!'

'Beg away, you honey-skinned bitch, it's music to my ears.' He swung a stunning blow across her mouth, bruising her lip against her teeth. 'And lie still, unless you want to be hurt more than is necessary.'

'Adone, you're behaving like a crazy person —oh God, stop it!'

'Yes, I'm crazy for you, but you like a man to keep his distance and not take liberties— how do you like this little liberty, eh?' Donna cringed from his touch, sickened and horrified by the animal he had turned into. Even his face seemed changed as he leaned over her and she felt his hand moving down her body. Adone! This was handsome Adone, for whom she had felt an affection because he was part of Rick?

Digging her fingers into the carpet in order to find strength and leverage, Donna waited to gauge the exact moment when he would be vulnerable enough for her to make a final effort to throw him off her body. When she felt the slight lifting and the fumbling she brought up her right knee and used it without conscience or care. She drove her knee into him and it was music to her ears when he cried out and his grip slackened on her. Quick as a flash Donna rolled free of him and leapt to her feet, racing to the door with a desperation such as she had never known in her life. She found the handle and could hear her own sobbing breath as she wrenched the door open and sped across the hall to the stairs.

It wasn't until she reached the gallery that she realised how torn and gaping her dress was. She drew the torn pieces against her and she was trembling from head to foot, and there was a stinging pain in her lips. Also there was an ache in her leg as if she had wrenched the calf muscle in her defensive action against Adone.

She swayed from sudden reaction and clung

to the scrolled ironwork that balustraded the gallery. What in the name of God had got into Adone to make him behave with such indescribable fury? It was as if something evil had overcome his charm and split him into two separate men, and Donna realised with a shudder that she had almost been raped. A sob caught in her throat . . . it was probably true what they said in the law courts about rape, that it did often happen to a woman with a man she knew, as if unaware she triggered off some primitive spark of temper and lust without having the faintest notion that it could exist in someone whose company she had found pleasant.

Donna turned from the balustrade towards her apartment and then came to a faltering halt. Rick was standing there looking very tall, his eyes steely and grim through narrowed eyelids. Donna felt as if her heart turned over, for Rick's eyes were raking over her dishevelment and he was demanding to know what had happened to her.

Chapter Eight

'I—I fell over.' Donna dragged the torn section of her dress across her bare skin, the strap of her net brassiere having been broken. 'It must have been quite a fall.' He took a step towards her, and still in the throes of deep sexual fear she retreated from him, her eyes widening with the distress of a woman who had been manhandled.

'I left you with Adone.' Suddenly there was an ominous note in Rick's voice and his eyes were fixed upon her swollen lip. 'My good God——'

'Just let me alone, Rick,' she said tensely. 'Let me go to my room——'

'He did that to you?' Rick's eyes were suddenly molten with rage. 'He abused you——?'

'Please, I want to go to my room.' Donna went to pass him, catching a frightened breath when he moved into her path. 'We had a quarrel, that's all. He tore my dress, but I—

180

I don't think he meant to.'

'He struck you—or did he do that to your mouth with a kiss you didn't want?'

'I fell a-and knocked my face. Rick, I want to go and change my dress.'

'My dear girl, don't defend the brute if he has done this to you!'

Donna stared at Rick and for the first time she understood why he disliked Adone, even though there wasn't a scrap of doubt in her mind that they shared the same blood line. He had told her there was a wild streak in Adone, and he knew just by looking at the state she was in that she had fallen a victim to it.

'What has he tried to do to you?' Rick moved another step nearer to her. 'It's all right, child, I'm not going to touch you, but if Adone has harmed you then I'm going to thrash the devil out of him once and for all. Tell me, Donna!'

'I made a silly remark and made him lose his temper.' Above all she didn't want Rick to lose his temper completely, for there was a strength in his shoulders and hands that the younger man could never match and he'd near enough kill Adone if he went for him. 'Please forget about it. I'm going to ask Serafina to release me from the job and I've decided to leave the villa as soon as possible. It's the best way—all round.'

'You can't leave!' A twist of sheer savagery

went across Rick's face, and even as Donna's heart gave a jolt between alarm and female awareness of why he didn't want her to go, she couldn't help but wonder if Adone inherited from Rick that untamed impulse he had let loose on her. 'I won't let you run away from that little swine! You don't have to——'

'I do, Rick.' She went to move past him, but suddenly her legs felt useless as she brushed against him and with a low exclamation he caught hold of her and swept her into his arms. He carried her into her bedroom and kicked the door shut behind him, and he held her close in his arms, his face buried in the side of her neck.

'I'll kill him if he's had his way with you! I've got to know, Donna, for the sake of my sanity!'

'No—he didn't get that far.' She was trembling again and wasn't sure if she was afraid of Rick . . . oh no, she couldn't blame Rick for the devilment in Adone, and almost of their own accord her arms crept about his neck and she clung to him, feeling the hard bone and strength of him, the protectiveness she needed so desperately right now.

'Things are getting out of hand,' she said shakily. 'Adone got upset because I talked to him about his engagement—Serafina told me about it, but I didn't dream he'd get so—so angry. He doesn't want the girl——'

'No, he wants you!' Rick spoke harshly even as he cradled her in his arms. 'You're a new kind of toy he wishes to possess and break in his destructive hands, but I'll break his hands if he ever touches you again!'

'Rick,' her hand moved to his hair and stroked his nape, 'I can't stay at the villa. Surely you must see that?'

'I can't let you go, surely you must realise that?'

'You aren't being reasonable,' she protested. 'You have Serafina to consider—we both know it and there's no way to ignore it. She owns you body and soul.'

'Do you really believe that?' Anger strained through the pain in his voice. 'Do you think I'm just an older edition of Adone, who wants you here for no other purpose than to besmirch your reserve and decency? Oh yes, in a way I understand what you do to him! Those with corruptness in them always want to drag what's sweet and clean through their own mud. It's a basic drive they're incapable of controlling. More and more it's in people these days, in those who produce films, who write plays and books and are enabled to communicate their infernal nastiness to others because some dirt merchant provides them with a shop window. How often these days does a man meet a young woman who actually has self-respect?'

Rick moved his hard jaw against Donna's

soft face. 'It's like finding a diamond on the edge of a drainhole. Never again must you be alone with Adone—do you hear me?'

'I'm leaving, Rick—please listen to me——' But his mouth had covered hers, silencing further words, drowning them in his kiss. He hurt her bruised lip, but even stronger was the charge of love right through her body, deep into its most sensitive areas. Her mouth softened, yielded beneath his, and her head fell back against his arm and everything was forgotten for endless moments. Donna's only awareness was that if Rick had ever been driven to a desire beyond his conscience she would have been powerless to resist him. She loved the feel of him against her . . . no single part of her body was repulsed by his.

'Don't leave me yet awhile,' he spoke in a rough whisper against her mouth. 'I never beg of anyone, but stay until we have to say goodbye.'

Goodbye . . . that most bleak of words, putting cold distance between people who longed for warm proximity. Hating the word and all it implied, Donna tightened her arms about Rick and his face sank down and buried itself near her heart, where her body softly curved and quivered at the touch of his warm lips.

'*Madonna mia, mia adorata,* you can't know, and I can't tell you, what loneliness I feel just to say the word. Stay, my heart. I will ensure that Adone never troubles you again. It's a firm promise, my dear. I never break my promises once they are made.'

She lay still in his arms, but her heart raced in her body . . . not away from Rick but towards him. It was without a ray of hope, but she had to stay because he asked her to. She had to give in to her heart even as her mind mocked her for a fool . . . a fool who knew that his nights belonged to Serafina and that snatched moments during the day could only be hers.

'You won't refuse me, Donna?' His breath rasped warm across her half-closed eyes. 'I shall see to it that you aren't frightened again by Adone.'

Her eyes opened then and clung to his, looking deep into their darkness where tiny flames burned.

'Rick, don't touch him, will you? There isn't any need, a-and it might cause trouble between you and Serafina. You know she dotes on him.'

'Yes, and it hasn't been to his advantage.' Rick held her gaze and a gleam of curiosity came into his eyes. 'Why isn't there any need for me to give him a well-deserved beating?'

'I—I used my knee on him, and from the yell he gave I believe I scored a bull's eye.'

Rick flung back his head and gave a yelp of laughter. '*Bella,* that should put him off his stroke for a while!' Then, sobering, he cupped her face in his hand and studied her every feature. 'You will stay, eh?'

'I shouldn't, Rick. If I had a scrap of sense I'd pack my bags today and leave before anything else happens. What if we ever got caught together like this—you in my room?'

'*Che disastro!*' And with a sigh he drew his hands slowly away from her and allowed her to leave his arms. He glanced around her bedroom, taking in the attractive simplicity of its furnishings. 'So pleasant and quiet here, no frills and heady scents of beauty lotions.'

'Only horses,' she said lightly. 'These rooms overlook the stables.'

'You don't mind that?'

'Not at all. I like the smell of horses and the sound of them in their stalls.'

'I must pick out a mount for you so you can go riding. We have some nice creatures— one of the mares is due to foal in a few days.' He pushed his hands into the pockets of his trousers and at the flick of his eyes Donna drew together the torn front of her dress, trying to look casual about it but intensely aware of the impulse Rick was resisting. She felt the flow of warmth over her skin, the tingling of her nerve ends for the touch that ached in his eyes.

'For your sake, Donna, I shall refrain from breaking Adone's jaw, but it would give me pleasure.' His eyes swept her up and down in her torn dress, his own jaw like a thing of iron. 'The sooner he is tied down with a wife the better. It will be arranged without delay, though I pity the girl!'

Rick strode to the door and there he turned and gave Donna a brief, rather grave smile. 'Until we meet again, eh?'

She nodded, and when the door had closed behind him drew off her ruined dress and put on a robe. She rubbed cold cream into her sore lip and combed the tangles out of her hair.

A feeling of weariness crept over her and she curled down on her bed, one arm flung across the pillow as if for comfort. She ached bodily from the bruises Adone had inflicted upon her, but it was the aching inside her that was harder to bear. Her arm wrapped itself about the pillow and her slim body in the silky robe was alive with longing for Rick's complete love. She almost wished it had been he who had flung her down on the floor in order to possess her. It would have been less cruel, somehow, than imposing such restraint upon himself that he left her so nervously strung up that she was ready to leap out of her skin at the slightest noise or movement.

She had agreed to stay here, but it wasn't going to be easy. This was a house shadowed by events in the past, and those scars on Serafina's wrists were Rick's penance for wanting his freedom to run his club in Rome.

What would Serafina's reaction be if she

ever caught him making love to her secretary? So far he had restrained himself, but Donna knew each time he held her close to him that he came closer to throwing off that restraint . . . the strongest man was unable to hide his desire from a woman, and Donna smiled a little, unable to deny herself the pleasure of knowing she was desired.

But her smile slowly faded, for all she had in place of desire was the loneliness a girl never fully comprehended until she met a man who meant absolutely everything . . . whose touch and talk and entire personality held a magic never found in anyone else. A powerfully shared fascination. An emotional rapport of mind and body—soul and sex.

Donna wanted the hard holding of Rick's arms, his teasing, and his tough protection. Without them she was half a person, and tightening her arms about the pillow she felt her vulnerability and her fear of the future. Love was only a source of strength if it could be realised . . . hers never could be, for Rick was committed to a woman who would kill herself rather than live without him.

Came the soundless slide of tears down Donna's cheeks as she gave in to the trauma of the past hour; it helped to cry a little, and she dozed off to sleep with the tears still wet on her face, and when she awoke there was a tray awaiting her on the bedside table.

Feeling renewed and suddenly rather

hungry, she sat up, pushed the hair out of her eyes and reached for the tray. There were several covered dishes, one being a *pizza* which was still warm, and delicious with its cheese, tomatoes and anchovies baked together. She ate hungrily and poured coffee from the pot, adding plenty of sugar and sipping it with half-closed eyes. Her bare feet curled together at the delicious taste, and it was an added sweetness knowing that no one but Rick could have arranged that her lunch be served in the peace and quiet of her room. Dessert was one of her favourites, a luscious black-cherry tart with a layer of creamy custard under the latticed pastry, covering the cherries an inch thick.

'You darling,' she whispered, blushing a little at the absurdity of talking to him when he wasn't there. But he understood her feelings and knew she would have found it hellish having to eat at the same table with Adone, and later that day he managed to slip a note under her door which came as such a relief that she actually trembled as she read it. Adone had been packed off to stay with his fiancée's parents, for it was deemed about time the couple got acquainted with each other, and a long-distance telephone call to Florence had settled the matter. Isabeta would be eighteen in a very short while and Adone would then become her official escort, on hand to take her to the round of dances and entertainments that would be arranged for them prior to their marriage.

Donna breathed a sigh of relief, though she couldn't help but feel a certain pity for the girl whose parents had arranged that she marry a virtual stranger. There was every possibility that as a convent girl she might become smitten by Adone's good looks . . . for Donna those looks had become a golden mask over the face of a devil.

Was there any real hope that he would settle down to be a faithful husband? Donna hoped so for the girl's sake.

The next few days were pleasant and fairly busy ones, for Serafina was now in the Hollywood section of her book and she had many tales to tell of the film people with whom she had worked in those golden days when the film city had been at the height of its glory.

In relating these anecdotes Serafina didn't resort to the tape-recorder but acted them out for Donna, who couldn't help but fall under the spell of the actress in this woman, who had not only dramatic ability but was able to reveal the funny side to life in Hollywood as well as the excitement and the competitiveness.

Now and again Rick strolled in to watch the performance, and at these times Donna noticed a relaxation in him and a softened expression in his eyes, as if Serafina recalled for him a time in their relationship when they had been more carefee together.

Donna tried hard not to feel jealous of that relationship. She did her best to be objective about the emotional tangle in which they were snared and told herself it could only add to her experience as a woman to have loved a man who had such gallant strength. A lesser man would have taken advantage of such a situation, but there was in Rick a core of steel that Donna found rather awesome. She knew he would stand by Serafina no matter how desperately he might want to hold her in his arms. Sometimes without intention their eyes would meet, and Donna would feel a physical sensation so acute that her legs would tremble. She knew that with all his body Rick was reaching out for her without being able to touch her, and her own reaction was a mixture of joy and denial.

There were times when she wished he would slip a note beneath her door and ask her to meet him at the *trullo sovrano*. And when he kept his promise about providing her with a horse she hoped he would ride with her and they would go again to that little stone house and kiss each other.

But it never happened, and she rode alone. It was as if he had clamped irons on his feelings and was resolved never again to touch her ...to draw her slim body close to his strength, so achingly close as he took her lips in kisses that aroused her to such a sweet wild longing for mutual surrender.

There was a kind of agony to loving this man who had shown her a glimpse of heaven and then withdrawn himself from contact with her, and sometimes she felt she would have to leave the villa rather than endure another night under the same roof with him. She knew that his nights were often spent in Serafina's apartment, and there were mornings when Serafina dismissed the very thought of work and lay on her balcony, gazing out over the valley and the mountains with dreamy, slumbrous eyes. It was as if her feeling for Rick was so intense that it sapped her vitality and left her looking like some beautiful wraith.

Those zestful mornings, when La Neri was brimful of her Hollywood triumphs, were far less frequent than her indolent ones when she was disinclined to do anything but wear one of her glamorous peignoirs and buff her fingernails.

'Run away and amuse yourself,' she said lazily to Donna. 'You like to ride, and Rick tells me you have a good seat.'

'But we aren't getting on very quickly with the book,' Donna had to protest. 'I came here to work and——'

'Are you getting bored?' Serafina gave Donna a considering look, as if she half suspected what made her restless. 'You get your salary, my dear girl, whether you pound the typewriter or go for a canter. Many would say that you have a cushy time working for me.'

'It isn't that I'm ungrateful——'

'Then what is it, pray?' A mocking gleam showed itself in the jade-green eyes. 'Is there a young Englishman waiting impatiently for you, or have you some other reason for wanting to hurry my memoirs? Is there someone you don't like, or maybe someone you like a little too much? One of the men working at the villa, perhaps? Does he pester you, or can it be that he hardly takes notice of your existence?'

'I—I just feel guilty about taking money for work I'm not doing.' Donna's nerves felt as if they were stretched on live wires. 'I'm your typist, not a guest at the villa.'

'You should like being treated as a guest.' Serafina spoke more sharply. 'There are times when you mystify me, you English girl. Does your frosting hide fire, I wonder?' She yawned delicately and the golden slave bracelet moved on her arm, revealing the fine pale scars where she had slashed her wrists in order to stop Rick from leaving her.

In place of riding clothes Donna wore slim yellow slacks and a pale-tan shirt with a length of silk knotted casually about her throat. The days right now were *bel tempo,* with skies so blue and flawless above the mountains that Donna could see the glittering layers of ice on the high peaks, thrusting into

193

the sky above the valley that was richly terraced with grapevines.

Donna was greeted on her rides by the
workers in the wine valley and offered grapes
by the lean young men with flashing eyes. She
would accept the grapes with a smile and ride
on, for the last thing she wanted was to
become involved with another Latin . . . she
was having a hard enough time loving Rick
and wasn't the kind of girl to find consolation
with someone else. She preferred her own
company and that of Centurione, a young
horse with a very gracious nature, hand-picked
for her by Rick and that extra bit lovable because of it.

Inevitably she made friends with some of
the young girls who worked in the vineyards,
and one of them, whose name was Assunta,
was soon to be married and she invited Donna
to be a guest at the wedding. Donna was immediately intrigued by the idea of attending a
real Italian wedding, but she wondered if it
would be considered proper for her to go
without an escort.

The next morning she casually asked Serafina if it would be all right, and to her
dismay was informed that if she went alone
she'd be swamped with eager young men who
would think she was available for all sorts of
attentions.

'You had better go with Rick,' added
Serafina.

Donna couldn't believe her ears, and Serafina laughed at the expression on her face.

'Don't you care for his company?' she asked.

'Of course——' Donna bit her lip. 'Why should I object?'

'Then why do you look as if you have swallowed an olive?'

'Would he agree to escort me to a village wedding?'

'If I ask him to do so. These village affairs hold no appeal for me, but now and again Rick has a nostalgia for the old ways of Sicily, and these rustic weddings are much alike, with great jars of wine, roast pig, confetti and almonds, and folk dancing. Rick will keep the eager boys from making a nuisance of themselves—you aren't the type who likes to be pestered in that way, eh?'

Donna shook her head, too dumbfounded to be offered Rick as an escort to be able to speak without stumbling all over her tongue. She couldn't imagine why Serafina was being so magnanimous and she didn't dare to ask . . . it was exciting beyond words, the thought of being with Rick at such a happy, carefree function as a wedding. Her heart raced at the prospect, though there was every chance he would refuse to take her, knowing how provocative it was when they found themselves thrown together.

That evening at dinner she tried to catch

his eye in order to silently appeal to him to take her to Assunta's wedding. To hell with her pride, she told herself. Serafina was going to have him to the bitter end, but all she asked was for one long, sunlit day in his company, among people who would sing about love and rejoice in its warmth and promise.

Serafina looked particularly stunning that evening, wearing a black silk-jersey dress, high-necked, with bands of silver beads down the sides of the long clinging sleeves. An exotic perfume clung to her, and her ear-clips were of jade clawed in gold, with a superb matching brooch on the shoulder of her dress. Her sophistication was complete, making Donna feel somehow naïve in a plain white dress trimmed with sea-blue.

It was while they were drinking coffee and liqueur in the *salotto* that Rick, standing over by the undraped windows in dark evening wear, suddenly looked directly at Donna across Serafina's dark smooth head. His eyelids seemed weighted with a hundred secret thoughts and his lashes threw shadows into the crevices of his lean face. He slowly lifted his glass to his lips and when he touched his lips to the glass Donna felt her heart move inside her . . . she knew in that instant that Rick was kissing her in his thoughts . . . making love to her until she lay helpless and weak in his powerful arms.

It was like an act of unfaithfulness right

there in Serafina's presence, yet defiantly she told herself she didn't care. She had little enough of him if he made love to her with his eyes it hurt no one but themselves.

'By the way,' Serafina drawled, 'I have suggested that Rick be your escort to this village wedding—and he has agreed.'

'Thank you,' Donna said quietly, and she didn't dare to look at Rick in case her eyes betrayed the golden tumult of her thoughts. Her eyes, she knew, had a tendency to turn gold when she was deeply excited, and with an air of sedateness she sipped her liqueur. She would find out from Assunta if she could borrow a regional dress from someone in the village and for one stolen day she would pretend to belong to Rick . . . to be his uncomplicated village girl.

Her heart told her that he wanted it that way as well, to forget for a day that he wasn't free to love her.

'Well, show Donna a little enthusiasm, *mio.*' Serafina turned her head to look at him. 'She will get the idea that you find it a tiresome bore taking her to this wedding.'

He quirked an eyebrow and then gave Donna an exaggerated genuflection, playing the mock Latin up to the hilt. 'Believe me, *signorina,* it will be a pleasure and an honour to be your escort, for I shall be the envy of every young man at the celebration. You will stand out like a white rose among carnations——'

'Don't overdo it, Rick.' Serafina gave a laugh with a sudden edge to it. 'You are making Donna blush with your Sicilian flattery. A white rose, indeed! Is that how she strikes you, *mio?*'

'She has fresh innocence, has she not?' He strolled to the piano and put back the lid. He sat down on the bench and ran his fingers along the keys. 'I am not Semprini, but I remember Sicily tonight and some of the island songs my mother taught me to play on the piano she had shipped all the way from Rome. My father muttered for days about the expense, but she only laughed at him and said she wanted her children——'

Rick broke off and began to play a tarantella, striking a few odd notes but producing a lively melody that made Donna's feet feel like dancing. Serafina had fallen into a brooding stillness, her lovely head at rest against a deep red cushion. Donna noticed that the liqueur glass was lax in her hand, and it came as no surprise when the glass suddenly slipped from her fingers and spilled its contents over the skirt of her jersey-silk dress. Serafina stared in a stricken way as the liqueur spread its stickiness through the silk, while Donna jumped to her feet and hurried across to see if she could help. To her dismay she saw tears gather in the green eyes and Serafina looked helpless and lost.

'Can I do anything?' Donna asked, tensing

as she felt Rick's hand press her shoulder and then withdraw. He leaned over Serafina and taking hold of her hands drew her to her feet.

'Come, there's no need to cry,' he said, and Donna watched as he led the weeping Serafina from the room. Donna felt mystified. Surely it took more than a spilled drink to make a grown woman cry like that, even if the drink did spoil a rather expensive dress? Donna slowly turned and gazed at the piano where Rick had sat and played a melody he remembered from his boyhood. Was that why Serafina wept, because she was moved by the music, and because she knew more about the tragedy in his life than anyone else? Was that why he was so gentle with her, treating her almost as if she were a child who had inadvertently spoiled her dress?

Deep in thought Donna wandered out on to the *terrazza* where the night air was redolent of cypress, lemon flowers, and a tumbling mass of wall roses. Overhead the sky blazed with countless stars and the *cigales* pulsed away in perfect beat. Donna felt strangely troubled, and also moved by the great gentleness with which Rick had led Serafina away, his arm about her waist, her head against his shoulder, the two of them sharing memories Donna could never be a part of.

She leaned against the *terrazza* wall and the tune of the tarantella kept beating away in her brain, and she knew beyond any doubt that she could never willingly cause a rift between Rick and the brilliant, moody actress who had been part of his life for so long. There was an affinity between them that left Donna out in the cold. It no longer warmed her that Rick desired her. Sensual hunger was only a part of love, and he had shared too many years with Serafina to let the passions of his body over-rule the compassions of his heart.

Donna bowed her head in thought . . . perhaps she shouldn't go with Rick to Assunta's wedding, where the atmosphere would be evocative of love and the giving of a woman unto a man.

She breathed cigarette smoke before Rick approached and came to stand beside her. 'Is Serafina all right?' she asked.

'Yes, she's taken a sleeping pill and gone to bed. She gets into these strung-up moods, especially now she's retired from the screen and has so little to do with her time. That was why I suggested she write this book about her career in films.'

'You suggested it, Rick?'

'Why not? She had a remarkable career and in many ways is a rare kind of woman, and a lot more courageous than you might imagine. It takes more than beauty to establish yourself in the hearts and minds of film buffs, and Serafina stayed at the top of her profession a lot longer than most. Now,' he drew hard on his cigarette and the tip glowed, throwing faint red shadows over his face, 'now she hasn't the release for her strong emotions that she once had.'

'She has you, Rick.'

'Yes, she has me.' He glanced absently at the stars. 'I think she realises that certain aspects of our relationship are hollow. I give her as much of myself as I can, but there are parts of me I can't give her. I wish to God——'

He broke off raggedly and Donna could feel him looking down sideways at her, moving his eyes over her hair which fell in a soft curve to her shoulder. She tensed and prayed he wouldn't touch her . . . she was jumpy herself and she might leap away if he touched her, or throw herself at him and find him more vulnerable tonight than he had ever been. She sensed in him a certain desperation that matched her own, and if Serafina had taken a sleeping pill she wouldn't want him tonight. It couldn't be wrong for two people to take each other . . . and yet Donna felt the shady, illicit wrongness in it; the awful chance to spoil what was somehow romantic and rather beautiful between Rick and herself.

Her gaze travelled upward to the stars, so pure, so lovely, so impossible to drag down into the mud. That was how she wanted her love to be, out of reach and yet as certain as those stars.

As Donna realised this, she also understood

that she was more grown up tonight than she had ever been, and deeply aware that the abiding seat of love was in her heart. She drew a soft sigh and watched a great white moth float by on gauzy wings . . . oh yes, now she truly loved and didn't need to gratify sensuality in order to feel its reality. She could look at Rick as she looked at the stars, and it was the most perfect feeling of her life.

'Why do you sigh?' he murmured.

'The night is so lovely—everything has a meaning, a purpose, even the smallest insect scurrying among those roses.'

'I thought you might feel sad.'

'No.' She shook her head. 'I think I've just become a woman, Rick. It happened without all that silly, specious nonsense in magazine stories about the raptures of the body. My heart is so alive and so aware. I'm part of you and you don't even have to touch me.'

'Ah, Donna——'

'No, don't touch me, Rick. This is the way it has to be with us and now I can bear it. It's even rather lovely.'

'We have the stars, eh?' A brief smile moved on his mouth. 'We mustn't howl for the moon.'

'You saw that film as well?' she smiled. 'It made me weep, but I didn't believe at the time that two people could care so much and yet walk away from each other—but it can be done, can't it?'

'If it has to be done.' He ground the stub of his cigarette into shreds and dropped them to the paving of the *terrazza*. 'I'm taking you to that wedding, if you are thinking of making that sacrifice as well. I assure you Serafina won't mind.'

'Are you sure, Rick?'

'Of course. You shouldn't leave Italy without attending an Italian wedding. It's all rather beautiful, in a warm, earthy, uninhibited way. Love should be like that—like fruits coming to season, like chicks breaking out of the egg, like rain falling on sunparched soil. A natural processs rather than the artificial one based on the idea that men and women are equal. *Per dio,* what man ever brought forth a baby? What woman ever designed a battleship? We are meant to be different and each in our own way important, one to the other. Therein lies the mystery and the excitement.'

'Oh, Rick,' Donna gave a soft laugh, 'you are very much a man, aren't you?'

'You are amused, eh? You find my ideas old-fashioned, chauvinistic, and out of touch with modern trends in living and loving?'

'No, I like them, Rick. They're a real man's logical thinking, and I hardly think you're the type to want a woman at your knees, pulling off your boots and kissing your feet.'

'The tail-end of what you say has an intriguing slant to it,' he drawled.

203

'Rick!'

'Has it not? The poor feet are just regarded as being there to stop us falling over, but really they have a lot of sensitivity in them.'

'I giggle when anyone touches mine!'

'Ah, and who, may I ask, has touched your feet with those curving insteps and slim ankles?'

Donna caught the rasp of jealousy in his voice and once again she was swept by the incredibly sweet awareness that Rick wanted her . . . that he had noticed so much about her, from her ankles to her eyes. She shivered with the secret delight of it, but Rick thought she was cold.

'Shall we go indoors?' he asked.

'No, let's stay a little while longer out here under the stars. Oh, what a night—what a lovely night!'

'You haven't told me who had the audacity to touch your feet.' He spoke into her ear, his breath moving warm and smoky against her skin.

'Who else but my dad?' she laughed. 'We were very close because we lost my mother when I was so young and needed double helpings of love. Rick, we have that in common, in a way.'

'Yes,' he said thoughtfully. 'We have much in common, *mi amore*. We look at the stars together and we really see them and know they are the eyes of heaven. We have affinity ——'

Donna caught her breath and Rick slid his arm about her waist. She had thought that he had affinity with Serafina, but was it really so? Had he ever been like this with her, able to relax and be himself; able to say deep meaningful things to which she listened? Donna glanced up at Rick and saw his profile outlined strong and remote against the starlight, as if he might be thinking the same thing as herself, that for much of his life he had worshipped at the shrine of Serafina's physical beauty and never found with her a comunication of the spirit.

'Yes,' he murmured, 'we have affinity, you and I. We knew it that night in Rome, and when we danced together, both of us masked, and yet in our hearts unmasked.'

He glanced down at her and the shattering tenderness in his smile went through Donna like a shaft of ecstasy, overwhelming her, making her weak and strong at one and the same time. To be with Rick was to be alive and aware as she had never been before, a part of him even though they might never experience ultimate union.

'In the strangest way,' she said softly, 'I have never been happier than I am right now. I'm glad we met, Rick. I'm so glad I won't go through life never having known a man who fits all my ideas of what a chevalier should be.'

'Many would smile at you for saying that,' he drawled, with a touch of irony, though she felt his hand press warm and hard against her body. 'I have a tough, hard reputation, Donna. I killed a man, though they called it justifiable manslaughter, and I carry a gun for a former *femme fatale* of the films. Where is the knight errantry in that, eh?'

'I know it's there and I don't care two hoots what other people say or think.' She studied his face and it was the rugged, uncompromising face of a man who had lived hard and suffered a wrecked boyhood. There were emotional scars no woman could hope to erase completely, but Donna knew she had touched his heart, perhaps with her youth, her romanticism and her innocence, and it thrilled her to the very core that she could make this tough man tremble when he drew her close and touched his mouth to hers.

They were lost in that kiss when a voice broke in on them, demanding Rick's attention. They tensed in each other's arms and though Rick's mouth ceased its warm caressive movements against her own, for a convulsive moment he was unable to relax his hold on her slim body. Then she felt a kind of shudder go through him and when he swung round to confront the owner of the voice he attempted to shield Donna as much as possible.

'What is it?' he asked, and he still breathed

unevenly. 'What do you want me for?'

He sounded half savage, like a man who had been dragged from the warmth of a dream.

Chapter Nine

Donna recognised the man as one of the stable hands, but his Italian was too rapid for her shaken senses to take in. Rick responded in the same rapid way, and when the man hurried away Rick turned to Donna and told her that his favourite mare, Contessa, was about to have her foal and he suggested that she go off to bed because he was going to assist at the birth.

'I was born a farmer's boy, as you know,' he said quizzically. 'My skills are various.'

'Mayn't I help in some way?' Donna looked eager, for she knew Contessa and sometimes spoiled her with a piece of sugar; a lovely chestnut who had been mated with Rick's bay stallion. 'I promise not to get in your way.'

'Have you ever watched such a procedure before?' Rick looked hesitant. 'Contessa is a thoroughbred and somewhat highly strung, and this is her first foal. Are you sure you want to be present? It isn't something to shrink from, but on the other hand you are——' He smiled slightly and moved his hands in an expressive way.

'I know what you mean.' She smiled herself. 'I'm a virgin who's supposed to get the vapours at the facts of life.'

'It isn't that entirely,' he shrugged his broad shoulders, 'but you aren't a country girl and you might feel a certain distress. Mares are like women, you know—they scream a little at these times, which is perfectly understandable, and you might find it rather hard to take.'

'Let me be with you, Rick.' Donna moved her hand against his arm. 'Time's running short for us and this is something special for you. I would like to share something like this with you.'

'Very well, but if you decide to faint do it on a bale of hay.'

She laughed, but knew the experience was going to have its harrowing moments as well as its wonders. 'Thank you, Rick, for being the man you are—for not treating me like a child.'

'You are a woman.' His hand touched her hair. 'Come along!'

The birth had its moments of difficulty, but the crisis for Donna, the testing moment for her, was when the mare thrashed out and caught Rick in the upper left arm with one of her hooves. Donna bit her lip in order to suppress a cry when she saw the blood quickly stain his white shirt.

'Hold her head,' he ordered, and Donna obeyed him, for the mare seemed to respond to her touch and to quieten down a little when she caressed the damp chestnut skin. Contessa writhed in the final throes of birth and her pleading eyes seemed to look directly into Donna's, and then Rick gave a heave and the foal was free, and Donna felt the pounding of her own heart as Rick's sure strong hands completed their task.

'A *bella bambina,*' he said, his teeth hard and strong against his sweating skin. He wiped the foal with a cloth and its coat emerged as creamy-brown, the mare's ears pricking with excitement as she turned her head and caught the scent of her long-legged baby. 'Here you are, sweetheart,' Rick gently placed the foal near its mother. 'Now you may kiss your son.'

The mare gave a little nicker and her long tongue began its task of licking and caressing the foal. Donna watched and was unaware of the tears on her cheeks, and when she turned to Rick he was sloshing water over his face from a bucket, and again she caught her lip between her teeth as she noticed his reddened shirt sleeve. The stable lamps flickered, casting shadows about the warm stall that smelled of hay and horse sweat. The stable hand passed a long-necked bottle to Rick, who drank from it thirstily.

'Keep an eye on her, Cecco, but I think she'll be fine. Not too bad a time for her, eh?' He thrust the damp hair back from his brow and gave Contessa and her foal a fond look. 'She has a lovely foal—he might turn out a racer with those legs.'

Cecco grinned and then glanced at Donna. 'The *signorina* has good nerves,' he complimented her, speaking slowly so that she understood him.

'*Grazie,*' she said, but she wasn't quite sure how long her nerves were going to stand the sight of blood still seeping through Rick's sleeve. 'That arm must be attended to, Rick,' she added.

He glanced at his arm and took another swig of wine. 'Later on,' he said casually. 'Now, what shall we call Contessa's son? Donna, would you like to name him?'

'May I?' Her eyes widened with delight and locked with his, which held in their depths a glinting pleasure in what they had shared—the beauty and menace of birth, the primitive wonder of it all. That sharing had somehow intensified what Donna felt for this man, for tonight she had come very close to the warm, capable core of him which his tough exterior concealed from most people.

'It would make me very happy to have you name the foal,' he assured her. 'Do you need time to think about it?'

'No.' Donna shook her head and glanced

at the mare who was absorbed in her foal, having nuzzled him to his long, tremulous legs so that now he was pressed close to her. 'May he be called Domino?'

There was a brief silence and when she looked at Rick she saw the big vein beating visibly in his neck beneath the sheen of his brown skin. He reached a hand towards her as if to touch her, then drew it back and clenched his fist against his thigh. He inclined his head and Donna could tell from his eyes that he was remembering that night in Rome when they had first spoken and danced in the Domino Room. She hadn't known then that he was bound to another woman, and she wondered if she would still have come to the Villa Imperatore had she known that Serafina Neri was that woman.

'Domino is the perfect name,' he said, and he walked over to Contessa and fondled her beautiful head. 'Do you hear, my lady, your son is named after a memory, and that is one of the nicest ways to be named.'

Donna felt a warm prickling of tears in her eyes . . . tonight would be safely locked away in her memory, for she could never love Rick more than she did right now. 'You must have that arm seen to,' she swallowed the huskiness from her voice. 'It's bleeding badly and needs bathing.'

He nodded, had a few words with Cecco, and then they made their way to the house.

The night air was cooler, the stars clear cut, and everything was wonderfully still. When they entered the hall Rick drew his jacket from her shoulders. 'You run along to bed, Donna. Your eyes are aching for sleep and I can manage to put a plaster on my arm.'

'Do you really think I'd let you slap a plaster on that cut without seeing to it properly?' Donna gave him a chiding look. 'You deserve more than that after what you've done tonight.'

'It isn't the first time I've helped a young animal into the world, and it won't be the last.' He gave her a quizzical smile. 'Domino, eh? I'm glad you thought of that, for when he grows into a proud young colt I can look at him and be reminded by his name of a certain young woman who made my life rather special for a while.'

'Tonight was very special,' she murmured. 'I shan't ever forget it and I do thank you, Rick, for letting me see Domino come into the world. It was so—meaningful.'

'Life, birth, all things ultimate have a beauty to them.' His eyes moved over her face, taking in the slight flush across her cheek-bones and the attractive disarray of her hair. 'You were good with Contessa, calm and tender. Animals are vulnerable creatures and not everyone is wise enough to know it.'

'Oh, Rick——' She saw what smouldered in his eyes and had to restrain herself from reaching out and clutching him . . . she knew that Rick ached for her as much as she ached for him; it was like a palpable heat coming off his skin and stealing over hers, a sensual feeling such as she had never dreamed of.

'I know, sweetheart. We shared something very intimate and earthy, and the natural conclusion would be for me to scoop you up in my arms and carry you to my room.' He drew a deep breath as if his heart was beating hard, and as her gaze slid across his chest she caught sight of his blood-stained sleeve and said quickly:

'Let me see to your arm—let me do that, at least?'

'Very well.' He glanced at the damp, clinging sleeve and grimaced. 'Who would have thought the old man had so much blood in him, eh?'

'You aren't old, Rick!'

'Years older than you, *carina*.' They mounted the stairs side by side and when they reached the gallery Donna made for the side on which her apartment was situated.

'There's a washbasin in my room, Rick, and I have some antiseptic.'

'Your room?' he murmured. 'I'm not that old, honey.'

Donna opened the door of her room as casually as possible, but she didn't dare to meet his eyes. She lit the oil lamps from the wall lighting filtering in from the gallery, and her heart gave a throb when Rick closed the door and they were alone together in the intimacy of her bedroom. He strolled to the padded bench at the foot of her bed and sat down on it, not saying a word as she went to the washbasin and ran water into it, and took from the little cupboard underneath a bottle of Dettol and a face-flannel still wrapped in a plastic bag.

'You had better remove your ~~skirt~~ shirt, Rick. I'll soak the blood out of it.' She managed with a certain effort to sound fairly casual.

'Anything you say, nurse.' She heard him give a slight, gravelly laugh and when she turned to him he was pulling the shirt out of his belt and stripping it from his shoulders. They loomed wide and brown above Donna as he came to her, rolling the shirt into a bundle and placing it at the side of the washbasin. The deep cut in his upper arm had ceased to bleed heavily, but the lips of it had a sore look, and he winced slightly as she applied the damp flannel with its application of antiseptic.

She bathed his arm intently but was conscious all the time of his gaze upon her, moving over her hair and her face. 'You missed your vocation,' he remarked. 'You have a firm but gentle touch.'

'This cut is quite deep, Rick,' she said, a note of concern in her voice. 'I do hope it doesn't become infected——'

'I'm tough as saddle leather,' he drawled.

'I'm thankful Contessa didn't lash out at you and dent your soft skin.'

When he said that it was as if he drew his hand over her skin, and Donna found it impossible to control a little shiver.

'It isn't that bad,' he laughed, but she felt his muscles go tense as she wiped the flannel over his skin, cleaning his arm of blood. Their eyes suddenly met and the naked need and yearning sprang like a flame from him to her. 'Oh God—you're right in my gut, Donna, and I want you—how I want you!'

She swallowed to ease her dry throat and turned to the cupboard for the packet of antiseptic plasters. 'I—I could make some coffee —I feel terribly thirsty. How about you, Rick?'

He nodded and she could feel his uneven breathing as she placed a pink square of plaster over the cut.

'There, how does that feel?' She glanced up at him, and bared to the waist as he was, with his tousled dark hair and that small gleaming ring in his earlobe, he had a pagan look that she both loved and feared with every scrap of her femininity.

'You look like a Sicilian pirate,' she said, catching her breath.

'I feel like one,' he growled. 'It wouldn't take much for me to scuttle my good resolutions right now and set sail for damnation. They say hell is paved with them, but it would be heaven—ah no!' He turned away with a groan. 'I'm tied, and there's no way for us to be together the way you deserve to be with a man—like that girl Assunta, who will stand at the altar with her young man and have it all made right, the way it should be.'

Tied! The word flashed at Donna and she flinched from it as she ran the stained water from the washbasin and refilled it with cold clear water in which she placed his bloodied shirt. She tidied the place, and then dried her hands on a towel.

'We could both do with some coffee—will you stay here, Rick, or shall I bring it to your room?'

'Not my room,' he said at once, and Donna bit her lip. His room was out of bounds to her because Serafina had access to it, day or night.

'I shan't be long.' She left him and went downstairs to the kitchen to percolate coffee and cut him some sandwiches. When she returned to her room with the tray Rick was sprawled on her bed, sound asleep, a large disturbing presence across the bedcover.

Donna set down the tray and stood there at the bedside looking at him, his features relaxed into vulnerability, tired out after his efforts on behalf of Contessa. She smiled a little. It seemed unfair to shake him awake just for the sake of drinking her coffee, and also she wanted to have him to herself just a while longer, and like this there was no harm in it. His brown chest moved with his regular breathing, shadowed by the hair across the firm muscles. His stomach was firm and flat, and Donna could understand how hard it would be for any woman to let go of this man.

Donna felt she wanted to bury her face in his chest and curl her body close to his and have for a little while the warm contact with him that couldn't last beyond tonight. Here in her room he had felt relaxed enough to fall asleep on her bed, and Donna realised the significance and was woman enough to resent that she must be but an interlude in his life who must give him up to another woman.

Her hand reached forward as if to shake him awake, but if she did so he would drink his coffee and leave her, and she would be alone once more. While he slept on her bed she possessed him . . . dark and big, grumbling sleepily as he settled into a more comfortable position.

Donna drew away from the bed and quietly carried the tray into the little *sala,* where she poured coffee for herself and sat drinking it. She would let Rick sleep on, and then towards dawn she would wake him so he could go to his own room and no one any the wiser that he had spent part of the night in her bedroom. That was her resolve, but the events of the night had made her sleepy and the little couch in the *sala* was hardly an inviting bed. Donna walked back into the bedroom and there she hesitated for only a few moments before slipping off her shoes and carefully lifting herself on to the bed beside Rick. As her head settled on the pillow she smiled a little . . . he'd be rueful in the morning when he found they had slept together in all innocence.

Donna woke suddenly and was instantly aware that a muscular arm was wrapped around her and had drawn her close to Rick's warmth. She lay and savoured the sweet closeness and nuzzled her face to his chest . . . and then came down to earth with a chilling thud when someone spoke from the foot of the bed:

'The pair of you make a pretty picture . . . that blonde hair scattered over Rick's shoulder . . . it's like something out of a romantic movie!'

Donna went to raise herself and felt the strong arm tighten around her, telling her that Rick was awake, that he had heard what Serafina had said as she stood there with her dark hair flowing about the shoulders of a jade-green velvet robe.

Rick's arm relaxed from Donna's waist and it was he who sat up, a hand thrusting the tousled black hair from his eyes, 'I know what you're thinking, *cara,* but this is all quite innocent. You should know me well enough by now to believe that I'd never seduce this girl, least of all under your roof.'

'Do I know you, Rick?' Serafina leaned her body against the bed, while Donna sat up and drew herself defensively away from Rick, who belonged to this woman who had come to claim him, as she always would. A tremor ran through her when Serafina slid green eyes away from Rick and studied her, crouching there unable to hide her feeling of guilt. It was her fault, all this, for not waking Rick. Like a romantic idiot she had wanted to sleep beside him, and now she had made him look a libertine when all the time he was kind and gallant . . . a sob caught in Donna's throat.

'Don't blame Rick,' she said huskily. 'He was tired after the foal was born and he fell asleep on my bed, and I——'

'Are you in love with him?' Serafina asked quietly.

Her quietness was unexpected, for Donna had expected a wild flare of temper, daggered fingernails reaching for her eyes, anything but the note of resignation in Serafina's voice.

'Yes,' Donna said, for now she had nothing to hide. 'I love Rick with all my heart, but I know he belongs to you and he has never at any time betrayed you——'

'Rick was always strong in ways that make other men weak.'

Serafina drew a sigh and then a faint smile

220

touched her mouth as she came to where Rick was still tensed upon the bed. She reached for him and cradled his face in her hands, and bending over him she laid a kiss against his hard cheek.

'Rick was always the best of brothers,' she said. 'Without him I would have ended my life long ago . . . *Cristo dio,* what I have done to you, *mio,* selfishly holding on to you and always putting my desires before yours, believing you were like the stone knight in my courtyard who could go through life without needing someone you could love as a man and not as a brother? Riccardo *mio,* how have you managed not to hate me?'

Donna heard these words with a stunning clarity and as their meaning struck at her heart she gave a little cry, and Rick turned to her once and caught her back in his arms, enfolding her close to the very core of him.

'It's quite true,' he murmured. 'Serafina is my sister, but not a soul beyond this room knows of it.'

'But why——?' Donna looked at Serafina with bewildered eyes. 'I just don't understand.'

'Few people would, if they were not Sicilian, if they had not suffered as Rick and I suffered all those years ago.' Serafina began to walk back and forth, beautiful with her flowing hair and yet with a sudden look of pain that made her seem haggard. 'How do I speak of it even yet . . . the torment, the horror, the desperate yearning to die that Rick would not allow? He carried me to the nuns and they cared for me—don't you understand, Donna, those awful men came to the farm and they killed our mother and they raped me—raped me!'

Rick gently let go of Donna and slid from the bed. He went to his sister and drew her against his shoulder, and in that instant Donna saw and understood the difference in his attitude towards his beautiful, tormented sister. She saw the protectiveness and realised it had always been in evidence whenever she had seen him with Serafina. The caring and the guardianship, and the total lack of anything sensual.

As he held her, his eyes found Donna. 'No one knows that we are brother and sister, that Serafina was long ago the young Lordetti girl whom the Mafia abused. For years we managed to hide it so that she might be the idealised screen star—it hurt no one, and I hardly cared that people thought of me as gigolo as well as bodyguard. No young girl was ever prettier than Sera, as we called her in those days, and then four thugs came to the farmhouse and I arrived home from rabbit hunting and found my mother dead and my sister in the mud of the yard where she had crawled to the water pump in an effort to wash off the feel of their filthy hands. They had almost brutalised the life out of her, my young sister of fifteen, and she begged to die. But she was all I had, and I took her to the nuns and they looked after her—until her baby was born.'

'Oh, no!' Donna's face went white as the bed sheets.

'Adone,' he said quietly. 'He knows of his illegitimacy, but he's unaware that his father was a Mafia henchman, whom I have always hoped was the one I disposed of in the age-old way of Sicily—by vendetta, by revenge. The other three were caught by the police, but the fourth had managed to elude them and I swore I would get him—and I did, and I was well aware that he was dead before he fell against the stone bollard which they allowed to be called his instrument of death. It is understood in Italy that certain passions must be revenged, but we are also Catholic, and Sera's baby had to come into the world despite the way he had been forced upon her.'

Rick drew a deep sigh and the lines were deeply incised in his face. 'We have always known that Adone might have characteristics not to our liking, but what can really be done about it? When all is said and done he is my nephew.'

Rick's nephew . . . Donna sighed softly to herself, and at last she understood why she had seen a resemblance to Rick in the handsome, rather decadent face of Adone. It would be there, for Rick was his uncle . . .

Rick was the brother of La Neri who all these years had been haunted by a terrible memory, and had clung to her brother in such dependence upon his strength and loyalty that she had found it impossible to live without him. Donna had never forgotten what her own father had once said to her, that if she ever found gallantry and sacrifice in a man she was to pay it homage, for it was a rare thing to find in this age of hardened hearts and debased values, with so many people making their selfish contribution to a dark age of lovelessness.

If Donna had loved Rick before this revelation she now adored him, and it was there on her face, there in her eyes, until she realised that Serafina was gazing at her with the sad eyes of a woman who had never been able to love since that traumatic day when on the threshold of life's sweet discoveries she had been brutally used by four adult men and left half alive for Rick to find.

'After Adone's birth,' he said, 'we invented the story of Serafina's marriage to an older man, which somehow suited the image of a girl rising in the film world. It was what Sera wanted, to be an actress, and it was what Sera achieved. It compensated, just a little.'

'And what of you, *mio?* What of you and your compensations?' Serafina drew herself out of his arms and took a long look at his lean, tough face which had never been

224

smoothed by the loving hands of a woman he could take into his life ... the life he had willingly devoted to the sister whom men had savaged.

'I've been unutterably selfish, Rick.' A shudder of self-reproach swept the shapely body that all these years had been worshipped by men only from a distance. 'I thought that because I could live without love, you also could live as a monk. Ah, I realise of course that there have been fleeting affairs of no account, but this time——' Serafina swept a hand in Donna's direction. 'This time, brother, you have met your blonde Nemesis, eh?'

'Donna understands the situation——'

'Does she really?' Serafina gave a soft laugh. 'I think I have suspected for some time that you were attracted to each other, but I thought it would flare, be assuaged, and then forgotten. But I came looking for you here when I found your own bed unoccupied, a man and a girl lost in each other's arms like the babes in the wood. I was very much moved, my dear Rick. I could see at once that it was something special, this young girl cradled in your arms as if she were the most precious thing in your life.'

Then, as a sob caught audibly in Donna's throat, Serafina lifted a hand to Rick's face and stroked his cheek. 'You have earned your grail, my perfect knight. You have been the very best of brothers and I have taken already too many years of your life away from you, making of you my guard against the night and the memories. You must have your Donna, and you must have babies with her, as a man is meant to—a man such as you. Few people know of the tenderness that burns in you, Rick, but it mustn't be suppressed any longer until it grows cool and the flame finally goes out.'

She turned and beckoned to Donna, who slid from the bed and came to her. Serafina took hold of her hand and then took hold of Rick's and with a smile she joined them together. 'I give my brother to you, Donna Lovelace. Love him—love him with your heart, your body and your soul, for he's one of the best of Sicilian men.'

Rick's hand tightened on Donna's, but his eyes were searching his sister's face and Donna sensed at once what was troubling him. Once before when he had wanted his freedom to go his own way Serafina had cut the veins in her wrists, using the blade from his razor.

'You tell me I can have Donna,' he said, 'but what are you going to do, Sera?'

'I am going to Rome.' With a sudden smile she drew something that crackled from the deep pocket of her robe. 'I have here a telegram from Elio Renaldo, who directed *There Shall Be No Dawn* about a year ago. It received very flattering reviews from the best critics, and now he wires me to ask if I will return to the screen to play the part of the mother in a film to be called *Sweet Calvary,* which he assures me has a marvellous script. I know what you are thinking, Rick, that I have never played a maternal part in a film because I've always liked to look glamorous. But I am a mother, after all, and will no doubt be inevitably a grandmother when Adone marries this young girl—and I am going to see to it that he does marry her!'

Rick's fingers were hurting Donna's, but she bore the pain with a pounding heart and could hardly believe that heaven might be hers . . . if Serafina truly meant to try and live her life without his constant surveillance.

'I mean to do it, Rick.' Serafina drew herself up straight and looked him proudly in the eye. 'I have missed film life more than I've admitted even to you, and that's one of the reasons why I've been unable to sleep and have taken too many of those damned pills, as you call them. I never needed them when I could exhaust myself on the film set, and if I make a success of this comeback, Renaldo will use me again.'

She was glowing, beautiful, and all at once Donna felt the tension slacken its hold on Rick's body. 'I should like more than anything to marry Donna,' he said, his voice deep with feeling. 'I loved her from the moment I looked at her, and she honours me by loving me in return.'

'Honours you, Rick?' Serafina laughed gently. 'My dear brother, I am sure Donna knows that she is the one who is honoured. Now I'm going to telephone Renaldo and to have a facial massage—don't stay too long in Donna's bedroom or the servants will gossip.'

When the door had closed behind her—and Donna felt sure Serafina had never in her career made such a perfect exit—she and Rick turned to look at each other for a long breathless moment.

'It can't be true,' he sighed. 'She will change her mind and I have always found it hard to resist her tears—she suffered so, poor young Sera, and was for weeks so apathetic that we thought her brain had given way from the shock she had suffered. Then the baby was born and there was no denying that he was beautiful like Sera, but she hated the very sight of him for a long time and he stayed with the nuns until he could be fostered with people we knew, closemouthed Sicilians who kept what they knew to themselves.'

Rick drew the breath harshly through his nostrils and went to where his jacket lay across a chair. He searched the pockets and found his cigarette case, and Donna watched, seated on the bench at the foot of the bed, as he lit a cigarette and drew the smoke deep in his lungs. 'I want you, Donna, you believe that?'

'With all my heart,' she replied, and she could still feel herself trembling a little; was still emotionally stirred up and hardly able to believe that Rick might yet be hers. But she knew he was torn by doubts . . . that he had been for such a long time his sister's custodian that he couldn't yet take in the implications of being free of such a duty.

'I have to be sure,' he added, 'that Serafina isn't just acting. I'd never forgive myself if I took my happiness at the expense of hers—she has tried before now to kill herself.'

'I know, Rick, I've seen the scars on her wrists.'

'You are such a wise, sweet girl,' he said tenderly. 'You make no demands of your own and yet you are entitled to, for you know I love you—quite desperately. You could say that you come before my sister, but you don't.'

'I have not had my body torn and my dreams raped like Serafina,' Donna said quietly. 'I can understand why you've needed your strength and your tough yet rare grace of heart. Just to know you has been wonderful —just to think of being loved by you brings my heart into my throat. But it if isn't to be——'

'I must find out for certain.' In two strides he was standing over Donna and then he was lifting her to her feet. His arm locked itself about her waist and bending down to her he took her mouth in a long shaking kiss. 'I must speak alone with Sera. You will be all right, my heart?'

'Of course.' She smiled, but her heart was afraid. Serafina couldn't open the door of heaven and then slam it in their faces . . . she couldn't be that cruel.

Rick left her, closing the door firmly behind him. Donna sank down on the bed and let her body fall into the place where he had slept. She buried her face in the lingering male scent of him and clutched the pillow with her hands. Oh God, would Serafina have let her into that well-guarded secret if she hadn't meant Rick to believe that she was setting him free at last? Even Adone was unaware of the true relationship between Rick and his mother. So secretive had they been that it was likely that only the Sicilian nuns, the priest, and the people who had cared for Adone knew that Rick Lordetti was more than a bodyguard to La Neri. After he had searched and found the remaining killer and rapist he had then attached himself to his sister, and they had been together every since . . . but what now . . . oh God, what now?

In a little while Donna roused herself and went along to the bathroom to take a shower and change into fresh clothing. She felt the need of coffee and rang for some, then she went and sat on the balcony of her *sala,* but was feeling too restless to remain there. The stables! She would go and take a look at Contessa and the foal.

They were doing fine and Domino was busy suckling when Donna entered the warm stall. Contessa snuffed at Donna's skirt and accepted sugar lumps from her hand . . . and at that precise moment an electrical thrill and awareness ran through Donna and she turned quickly around and there was Rick, leaning with a shoulder against the wall, clad in a shadow-weave shirt with dark tailored trousers emphasising his length of leg.

He smiled invitingly into Donna's eyes and opened his arms to her. She ran swiftly to him and was collected so closely to him that she almost lost her breath.

'Serafina is packing right now to go to Rome,' he said, moving his lips against her face. 'She seems quite excited.'

'But won't she be nervous, Rick? She has depended on you such a lot and has this fear of being—attacked.'

'Renaldo is sending the company helicopter to pick her up, and it seems they employ really tough professionals to guard their stars.' Rick held Donna's eyes with his own and there was a deep down, very certain smile in them. 'I think seeing us together acted as a kind of release for Sera—let's say a little punch over the heart that made her realise that she can and must make it on her own. She knows I love you and that I must put you first—yes, my heart. Sera is my very dear sister, but you are my soul.'

'Oh, Rick——' Donna was lost for words and could only kiss his throat in the opening of his shirt and love every bone and sinew of him, now and into the limitless future.

'I shall make arrangements for us to be married quickly and quietly by the local priest, and we shall attend Assunta's wedding as man and wife. Would you like that?'

'With all my heart, Rick.'

'My Saxon girl.' He stroked loving fingers through her fair hair. 'This time, thank God, we escaped being torn apart.'

Donna smiled as his lips closed upon hers, and never would she forget that night in Rome, where she had met and loved her dark Sicilian with the ring of revenge in his ear. She touched the golden ring with her fingertip, and though she knew that Rick would never be totally rid of his terrible memories she would ensure that his future was filled with love.

The publishers hope that this Large Print Book has brought you pleasurable reading. Each title is designed to make the text as easy to see as possible. G. K. Hall Large Print Books are available from your library and your local bookstore. Or you can receive information on upcoming and current Large Print Books by mail and order directly from the publisher. Just send your name and address to:

G. K. Hall & Co.
70 Lincoln Street
Boston, Mass. 02111

or call, toll-free:

1-800-343-2806

A note on the text
Large print edition designed by
Fred Welden.
Composed in 16 pt English Times
on a Compugraphic II
by Cambridge Press, Inc.